UERTIGO

Also by Kristina Dunker

Summer Storm
The Birdcatcher (forthcoming)
Runaway (forthcoming)

VERTIGO

Kristina Dunker

Translated by Katja Bell

amazon crossing

Vertigo by Kristina Dunker was first published in 2007 by Deutscher
Taschenbuch Verlag GmbH & Co. KG in Munich as *Schwindel.*

Translated from the German by Katja Bell.
First published in English in 2012 by AmazonCrossing.

Published by AmazonCrossing
P.O. Box 400818
Las Vegas, NV 89140

ISBN-13: 9781611090482
ISBN-10: 1611090482
Library of Congress Control Number: 2011963583

VERTIGO

1

I was so happy. It was all so exciting.

Boy, I had no idea.

That Thursday, October fourth, the sky was wide and blue, like you only see it during early fall. Three buzzards circled high above the stubble field as I walked home from school at lunchtime. They made me ache for faraway places with their high-pitched cries. I might have wanted to run out onto the shimmering field of gold and fly my kite had I not been an almost-seventeen-year-old with very different things on her mind.

My heart beat faster thinking about the weekend ahead that I was to spend with my boyfriend; I lost my walking rhythm, stumbled. Chestnuts lay on the street, many of them still in their green, prickly skins with the shiny fruit inside trying to break free. And that's exactly how I felt, myself. A heart freed from its dragon hide, a body changing its skin, a soul in uproar—and all of this because of Julian.

It had only been six weeks since he and I bumped into each other in the school hallway, on the very first day after summer break. I was looking for my classroom and wanted to push open one of those glass doors connecting the hallways but it wouldn't budge, so I almost ran my head into the glass.

"Pull," said a tired voice beside me.

"Sorry, it's my first day."

"Mine too." Big yawn. "I almost forgot all about this stupid place during summer break."

"This really is my first day," I explained. "Just moved. Today is my first day of school in every respect. All I need is one of those back-to-school goodie bags."

I have no idea why I would mention such a stupid thing as a back-to-school goodie bag. Sometimes ideas like that just pop into my head. I started regretting my remark immediately, but the boy seemed to think that it was quite original.

"And what would you want to have in your back-to-school goodie bag?" he asked, a little more awake now, and walked beside me as if we'd been friends for a long time. "Crayons and a recorder flute?"

"How about CDs and cigarettes?" I cocked my head to the side, unsure if he would like this reply, too. It certainly was pretty far from the truth. My computer is an old piece of junk, I still don't smoke to this day, I might have *some* use for crayons, and I'm also into making my own music.

The boy really started getting into this.

"Yeah, right, and a cell phone, a few computer games, some money, a little weed…"

He was nice looking: tall and athletic, tousled chestnut hair, eyes like big shiny blackberries, and a grin that makes you go soft in the knees. Yes, in fact, my knees were a little soft. But that didn't mean a thing; they sometimes are.

We had arrived in front of the tenth-grade classrooms. The boy greeted some of my new classmates.

"Nice back-to-school goodie bag. Awesome educational value," I said to him and laughed in his face, hoping maybe to make friends faster this way.

"Well, you know, keeping up with the times." He gave me a wink. "I'm Julian, I'm in twelfth grade. Maybe I'll see you around."

"Yeah, maybe." We maintained eye contact for a few seconds longer than necessary. I immediately knew that I liked him, which was irritating because this is not something that happens to me with a lot of people. Maybe with my friend, Sarah, whom I had met on vacation at a campground by the Baltic Sea; and maybe a little also with the fox guy who—as he opened the door for me for the first time—smiled at me in such a disarmingly open and curious way that I forgot all about being shy and just opened up to him.

So, "like" at first sight, sure; but the famous "love"? No way! No, I did not believe for one second that I would speak to Julian again. I just didn't feel that I was interesting enough for a boy who was two years my senior, who had been living here for a long time, and who surely had a girlfriend.

But in fact we did meet again—during recess, to be precise. He stood next to me while I was waiting in line at the school snack store, called me "goodie bag," and politely asked to go first as if it was a given.

"Your boyfriend?" the girls from my class asked straightaway and not at all discreetly so that Julian—who now stood in front of us by the counter—overheard us.

Julian shook his head. "We only met this morning." Then he turned around. "But who knows? Things can always change."

"Hey, listen to that!" The girls were enthused. I barely noticed them, looked at Julian. His quick-witted remark seemed to have surprised even him; he tried to smooth over his terrified embarrassment, saying, "Just kidding, of course."

"Bummer." I don't know if I even said the word out loud, or if I just mouthed it silently with my lips, or if it only formed like a cartoon speech bubble inside my head. Because, you see, I cannot imagine ever saying anything so daring. Nonetheless, Julian received my message—maybe because of the way I looked at him or through telepathy, because as I grabbed the sales counter to steady myself when I had a sudden dizzy spell, I grabbed his hand instead.

"Oops!" Julian laughed, blushing beautifully, while Vanessa, Verena, Vivien—and whatever else their names were—were thoroughly enjoying themselves.

"Uh, my name is Eva," I said.

"Adam!"

"Dumbass!" I squeezed his hand a little tighter, and although I was extremely embarrassed when one of the girls suddenly yelled, "You may now kiss the bride," an incredible feeling of being totally in love washed all over me and I really wished that he would.

Still, we did wait a few more days before timidly experimenting in an ice cream parlor to see whether our lips also tasted of chocolate chip and amarena cherry. After all, Julian was my first-ever boyfriend, and I really didn't want to rush into things.

On the other hand…I never really felt comfortable at my old school, never really had my own circle of friends, and I've been wishing for a boyfriend for a very long time. So why not go on vacation together, just the two of us, six weeks into our relationship? Something that started out this good could only keep getting better! Right?

Everything certainly seemed to point our way. We would spend the next four days in his parents' vacation home, a former water mill—as he described it to me—located in a very romantic setting on a tributary of the Mosel River. In this lovely warm weather, we would bathe in the ice-cold creek before breakfast, take a spin on Julian's motorcycle down winding country roads, and go shopping in historic downtown. In the evening, we'd have a barbecue, and later on we'd snuggle up on the super-soft rug with a suspense-filled movie, or simply lie in front of the fireplace and enjoy the luxury of having the whole entire night still ahead of us. Nobody there to disturb us. No worried moms, no inquisitive dads—the weekend at the Rauschenmühle water mill was to be all our own, and we planned to finally do what we've wanted to do all along but have been putting off.

I picked up one of those prickly chestnuts and closed my fist around it. To be honest, as much as I was looking forward to my upcoming trip, I also had a small case of the jitters.

Lately I was experiencing sudden little tugs around my belly button, goose bumps all over my body, and a barely suppressed desire to start screaming at the top of my lungs—as if I was on a roller-coaster ride rushing from the peak to the depths below. My parents noticed this, of course; I e-mailed Sarah all about it; and even the fox guy knew, calling it a pleasant fear, a very normal, blissful feeling of happiness. That's exactly what it was, of course. Sitting in front of my homework assignments, suddenly noticing Julian's wink, powerlessly sliding off my chair, and feeling like a stick of butter melting in the sun. Singing in the school choir and—during the staccato—thinking about Julian's fingers tickling my belly, and from then on having to break into laughter with every little move of my diaphragm. At night, waking up from an orange-red dream, arms and legs wrapped around my comforter as if it were *The One*.

This was when I accepted my excessive sensibility for the first time in my life. I had always thought of it as a disadvantage, as a taint and a shame, something that needed to be overcome. But now I was almost starting to like myself. The period of time from my meeting Julian for the first time until my leaving on this October fourth had been great, simply great, with everything seeming to work out perfectly all of a sudden. My parents almost—almost—stopped worrying about me. Even the fox guy seemed satisfied. He said that by the looks of it, I might soon be able to get by without him, which made me happy and touched me in a strange way all at the same time—because for one, I was arguably getting used to him; and for another, I sensed that maybe I had not yet overcome all of my fears, that I still had to face my crucible, my baptism of fire. I had no idea, of course, that I would have to face it during my weekend getaway with Julian, of all times.

2

When I got home, my dad welcomed me by saying, "Eva, be careful when you cross the hall, I pulled everything up in there. We're getting the new doors today."

He stood in front of a wallpaper-pasting table in the shade of the walnut tree, wearing his blue overalls. Two squirrels darted up the tree not two yards behind him. The brown one's fur reminded me of Julian's hair. The chestnut one was probably the female, and somewhere up in the canopy they had created their love nest. Lordy, I felt so good!

"What's with all the grinning? You could give me a hand, you know."

"No time. My train's at ten past one."

"Ah, so you are going?"

"Yeah, of course!" What else was I talking about and why else was I so happy this whole entire time?!

"Just saying. You feel fine and…"

"Yes!" I gritted my teeth.

"Okay, I think that's great and all. Mom is worried of course. In general, you know. I mean, after all, it's the first time you're going on vacation with your boyfriend all by yourself."

"Vacation? It's only four days!"

My dad laughed. "Still! *Some* people have to work. It's not as easy as I first thought to fix up Granddad's old house. Okay, so I'll drive you to the station in a minute. What time will you arrive at this Munkelbach place and the water mill?"

"Half past five. I have to change trains three times."

"Well, you're young. But you'll call us, remember!"

"Of course I will," I replied, going into the house. I threw my schoolbag into a corner, punched my trekking backpack—packed and ready—as I would a good friend, turned up the stereo, took a shower, made myself a kaiser roll with cheese, ate it in front of my open closet, and imagined my munching-crunching, mirror-posing self—top-model beautiful—getting off that train in Munkelbach and flying into my Julian's open arms; Julian, who would be waving and holding a bouquet of red roses.

Julian, as a senior, was a little more flexible when it came to managing his class schedule than I was, and so he had left on Tuesday afternoon—the day before the public holiday—while I had to attend a few more classes on Thursday, with Friday being my only day off, thanks to a teachers-only field trip. If those annoying four classes on Thursday morning had been cancelled or if my parents for once had been willing to write me an excuse, Julian and I would have had almost an entire week of vacation to ourselves. But Julian left for Munkelbach on Tuesday without me. Munkelbach, the murmuring creek. As far as I knew, he wanted to take advantage of the extra time to get some maintenance work done for his parents. I thought nothing of it. I liked my boyfriend's versatility, liked that he was part of a handball club, that he played the saxophone, and that he was obviously a skilled handyman. How could I have known that it might be a mistake not to go to Munkelbach together?

"Eva," my dad called, "it's time!"

"Coming!" A quick dash back into the bathroom to check my appearance: hair, top, sunglasses—check. I inspected my bags: cell phone, journal, birth control—check. I wrapped the denim jacket around my hips, shouldered my trekking backpack. All set!

Phew, let's go, and remember to stay cool!

As I hurried through the narrow hallway, my bulky backpack must have caught on that pulled-out doorframe. I felt the tug and heard the noise of something ripping or tearing, but I just kept on going and didn't check whether everything was still safe and sound in the side pockets where I stored the things that I wanted to keep handy.

3

My dad didn't follow me into the railroad station; he was too preoccupied with his little construction project. Before he let me out of the car, however, he was sure to reiterate all the essential pieces of advice I had listened to a million times already during the past few days.

"Yes, of course, I will look after myself! You can trust me," I interrupted and added amiably, "Can I bring you back anything nice from the Mosel Valley?"

"Do you have enough money?" He pulled out his wallet.

I never seemed to have enough of it these days. Must be because of Julian, who was extremely well taken care of when it came to pocket money.

My dad slipped me two more bills, hugged me.

"Okay, have fun."

I gave him a wave and entered the railroad station, heart pounding. For one thing, I was nervous, hurrying along more than necessary, feeling the paper of the train tickets curl in my sweaty palms, and touching my jeans pocket twice to make sure that my wallet was still there. For another, I was almost giddy. My eyes—I was able to see my reflection in a window—glowed big, like two polished, semiprecious gemstones. My cheeks were as shiny as the two waxed apples I had packed as my travel provisions, and when a woman accidentally rolled her suitcase over my foot, I simply replied to her apologies with a forgiving smile. What was a little pain in my foot? I was on my way to my Julian! I felt like jumping up into the air!

Only a few months ago I wouldn't have dreamed of going on vacation with my first steady boyfriend. I imagined that nobody liked me—not my classmates, who always excluded me; not our neighbor's daughters, who were right in the middle of puberty and would start giggling whenever I passed them in the entrance hall; not the volleyball coach, who put me back on the B team due to "certain issues"; not my parents, who had wished for a less complicated, more "able" daughter; and not even the fox guy, who, after all, got paid to spend an hour or so with me once a week.

But all this was behind me now! Since our move and since my first day at the new school, not only did I have Julian by my side, but I had also made a whole bunch of new friends. I had joined the school choir and given the volleyball club and all my old acquaintances the boot, and soon I would even be rid of the fox guy—who probably did like me a little after all, as I was beginning to realize.

Because now, you see, is when the sweet life begins! The arriving ICE train seemed like a promising white arrow to me, my direct connection to famous cloud nine. As my train stopped, softly creaking, and another train on the other side took off in the opposite direction, the ground beneath my feet swayed gently. What had the fox guy called this feeling? A very normal, blissful feeling of happiness.

And now, I was finally on my way!

It didn't take Julian a long time to call.

"Where are you now?"

"On the train, sitting on the floor."

"Why would you do that?"

"I couldn't get a seat, but that's okay." I felt the army soldier who was sitting opposite me in the crowded aisle prick up his ears. He had already smiled at me—twice—and pointed at a hot air balloon that you could see through the window. He now cocked his head to the side, rested it in one hand, and stared directly at me. This irritated me so much that I couldn't hear what Julian said next.

"I can barely understand you," I lied.

"I can't wait to see you!" Julian almost yelled.

Me too, is what I wanted to say, but I felt so stared at by this fellow passenger—who probably wanted to hear these same words from me as much as Julian—that I was totally tongue-tied.

"Eva?" Julian asked. "Hellooo?"

"The connection is really poor."

The soldier—who had *Berger* written on his uniform—smirked as if he was reading my thoughts. The way he acted reminded me of the fox guy, and that made me very nervous.

"Where are you right now? Will you be on time?"

"I think so. Well, the train left on time, I guess."

"Okay, but I'll try to call you again. See you soon!"

"Okay, bye." I turned off my cell phone.

My fellow passenger seemed to have listened to my entire conversation. He pointed at the electronic information panel above my head. "We're not really on time. According to the schedule we should be in Düsseldorf by now."

"That's only a few minutes late…!" Really not feeling like talking to him, I pulled my little green journal from one of the side pockets of my backpack and started leafing through it—with my head down, trying to make a point. I could feel Berger looking at me for a little while longer, and then he sighed in disappointment and finally turned to his buddy next to him.

That's something the fox guy would never have done. The fox guy never gave up quickly. Besides, he lived and breathed for conversations. And so the fox guy either would have asked me a question that I just *had* to answer, or he simply would have waited until I couldn't stand the silence any longer and started talking automatically. Well, with me this never took long. Even in the beginning, when I was still afraid of giving away too much of myself, the fox guy somehow always managed to get me talking.

But right now I wasn't in a contemplative mood. I was on the way to my vacation, to my Julian!

I relaxed, closed my eyes, and was daydreaming when the train conductor announced over the intercom that we would be arriving at Düsseldorf Central shortly, but seventeen minutes late, and that any connecting trains hadn't been able to wait.

"Hopefully, we'll make up for the delay by the time we get to Bonn," I mumbled, but I immediately realized from Berger's expression that this was pretty unlikely. So I took out my cell phone and dialed Julian's number. He didn't sound very happy when I told him that I might potentially miss my connecting train.

"But I might still make it," I said, hopeful, "and I will definitely run."

"Okay, well, if not—it's not so bad. You'll just arrive an hour later, that's all. Shame, but there's nothing we can do."

"Yup, we still have the entire weekend to ourselves."

"Exactly. Alright, let's not freak out just yet. We'll have a really nice time once you get here."

"Okay!" A delayed train really was no reason to worry.

"Ah, to be in love, to have a girlfriend," Private Berger said, grabbing his bags and standing up to say his good-byes. "Have a great weekend. I'm sure it'll be unforgettable."

That it certainly was.

At Bonn Central, I treated myself to a cappuccino, scribbled furiously in my journal, with my butt half-perched on a stool in a stand-up coffee bar, and tried to kill some time by leafing through everything that looked remotely interesting in the bookstore. When it was time to board my connecting train—the regional express train that I was supposed to have been on an hour ago—I overheard the announcer say that it would arrive twenty minutes late due to some mechanical problem.

"You've got to be kidding," I blurted out. This meant that I would also miss the little Lilliput train in Koblenz. Another hour lost!

I felt my fingers go all jittery as I reached for my cell phone. What would Julian say? Okay, it wasn't my fault that I would arrive much later than anticipated. But still!

"Hi, it's me. I'm in Bonn, which at least is something, but I mightn't get there until much later because I probably won't even make my next connection."

"You're kidding, right?"

"Um, no." I was feeling a little insecure and idly stared at the people rushing past me. "So, how's it going with you? Have you fixed the roof yet?"

"Not yet."

Sheesh, why was he being so snippy all of a sudden? Okay, so he didn't appreciate the timing, but what was he thinking? That I enjoyed spending all this time inside of railroad stations?

We were silent for a little while. Somebody bumped into me while hurrying past. I felt for my wallet. If that gets stolen now I'll be totally lost, I remember thinking.

"Okay, Evic, don't get yourself down. I'm sure you'll get here eventually. Either way I'll be waiting for you, even if it takes until tomorrow morning," Julian's voice then said, and the sudden feeling of very brief, very black despair lifted as quickly as it had come over me. I sat down on a bench, took in the afternoon sun, and again pulled my journal from my backpack. Where would I be without this great big piece of comfort?

During these past two years, I entrusted almost everything that was on my mind to this little book. It retold my life story in turquoise-colored ink (sometimes diluted with tears), reflected on my talks with the fox guy, confessed my deepest, most intimate secrets. Last night, I contemplated whether bringing it was the right thing to do. Julian, you see, had absolutely no idea what I was writing about all the time.

He never even bothered to take a look "behind the scenes." He wasn't surprised that I never introduced any of my old friends to him, and he never even asked how comfortable I had felt at my old school. I think he just couldn't imagine that I had been so miserable before the move; that six weeks into my new life I still thought it was all a nice dream from which I would wake up at any moment, and that I still needed outside help to cope with it all—despite all these awesome developments. Maybe, or so I hoped, being in Munkelbach together would give me the chance to open up to Julian, which meant that I would finally be able to trust my boyfriend—and no longer the fox guy who was, after all, a stranger.

I could picture it all on my way to Koblenz. Taking in the gorgeous scenery along the Rhine River only strengthened my sense of optimism: vineyards, old castles high up on the hilltops, the river shimmering gold under an Indian summer sun, trees and their warm blaze of colors reflecting in the water—everything was perfectly idyllic.

The sky was no longer bright blue when I arrived in Koblenz at around six o'clock, which is to say more than an hour and a half later than planned. And then I received two pieces of bad news at once. First, someone from Travel Information informed me that the local train to Munkelbach only ran every two hours, meaning that I would lose another hour. So I wouldn't get to Munkelbach until 7:38 p.m. instead of the original 4:38 p.m. No sooner had I told Julian the bad news and, feeling pretty down, treated myself to a hot chocolate, that Julian called me back and let the cat out of the bag, so to speak.

"Eva, listen, I have a little problem."

"What is it?" My voice had a nervous ring to it, even though that's exactly what I was trying to avoid.

"I had an accident."

"Whaaat?" I almost spilled my hot chocolate.

"Yeah, so this afternoon I was working on the shed roof, I jumped all the way down, and somehow I landed badly and twisted my ankle. I'm afraid I can't come and get you. I can't seem to put any weight on my foot right now."

"Do you think it's broken?"

"I don't know yet. Maybe I got lucky and just sprained the ankle. Anyway, I can't come. You'll get a taxi, okay?"

I so would have loved to plead with him: "But I've been traveling all day, please, please, come and get me! I need you to come get me, I'm totally beat!" I wanted to explain how tired, hungry, and exhausted I was, but I didn't. I couldn't allow myself to break down. After all, I didn't have a problem; I just had a beef with the German train system and its lack of punctuality. But he—he was injured!

"Not a problem, I'll get a taxi," I said slowly. "It's okay if you can't come and get me. Better get some rest. I'll look after you as soon as I get there, what do you say?"

"Oh yes please!" Julian purred like a kitten. "You know, Evie, we should try to have a really nice evening after all this bad luck the two of us had today. I'll open one of Dad's bottles of red wine and get a nice fire going."

"Great. Can't wait." I felt comforted by his words, even though I could barely picture myself ever getting to the Rauschenmühle water mill. Still, I tried to stay calm, took a big gulp of cocoa, and told myself that nothing would ruin my mood. Although, I might have a bit of a problem with the red wine.

4

At ten to seven the little local train finally left for Munkelbach, but it was very slow and creaked so much that I was worried it would never get anywhere but stop someplace along the tracks and break apart. It started getting dark outside. At first, I was still able to read the names of all the railroad stations we passed. But pretty soon, somewhere between Upper Lückendorf and Lower Lückendorf, the lettering became sketchy, and in the next backwater town I was only able to make out my own face in the window, along with a scarcely illuminated platform. Next, the conductor also stupidly stopped calling out each individual stop. For the love of God, what if I now missed Munkelbach! I scampered through an almost-empty train. Most of the people who had boarded in Koblenz carrying briefcases and shopping bags had gotten off by now. I ran into a girl with a good number of facial and body piercings.

"I'm also getting off at Munkelbach," she said sluggishly.

Relieved, I plopped down into the seat next to her, let my heavy backpack slide down from my shoulders onto the floor for the millionth time, yawned, felt the cocoa repeat on me, and thought to myself: If you're going to be nauseous and sick, then it's totally over and you may as well take the next train home—that is, if there is a train!

As if "next train home" had somehow made her ears burn, my mom called.

"Did you get there okay? Everything alright?"

"Not quite, but I should be there in about twenty minutes or so."

"What do you mean you're not there yet?" My mom suddenly sounded alarmed.

"Engine malfunction, high track usage rates, signal failure...take your pick; it was a little bit of everything."

"But you're okay?"

"Yes, Mom."

"Are you sure?"

"Of course!" I hissed at her. Sorry, but I'm so sick of all these stupid questions: Are you okay? Everything alright? You're so quiet—you're not brooding, are you?

Why did they *always* have to point out that I should be doing better and that there were people—people like her, or like my classmates—who had a better grip on life than I did?

"It's only normal that we're worried," my mom replied, a little irritated.

"Yeees." I stretched my words out deliberately and noticed that my cell phone battery was also running low on power and patience. No wonder, I had forgotten to charge it before I left, and after all of this back and forth, the battery was almost empty.

"Mom, I have to go. I'll call you as soon as I get to the water mill, okay?"

"Take care, honey."

This phrase always throws me off, whether I want it to or not.

I rested my face on the window and stared into my big, tired eyes in the reflection. Did I look anxious?

"You seem very anxious and insecure to me," the fox guy had said when we met for the first time.

"Munkelbach." The girl with the facial and body piercings got up.

"Thanks."

Just then, Julian called again.

"My battery's about to die," I said quickly. "I can't talk long, but I'm almost there."

"Okay, finally! Evie, promise me that you'll take a taxi, right?"

"What else?"

"I just never know with you," Julian countered, "you're always full of surprises."

I hesitated. Did he really mean *me*? Should I take this as a compliment?

"I hope it's only pleasant surprises," is what I wanted to say, and I did, but I'm not sure if he heard me. My battery was now definitely dead, and my connection was cut off.

To arrive all alone in a strange place—in the dark—is pretty depressing. I saw how piercing-girl flew into the arms of her boyfriend, who himself was tattooed all over; how she cuddled her bull terrier; and how the three of them went on their way. I saw the handful of people who had left the train at the same time as I did rush past me. In an instant I was all by myself on the platform, the train was leaving, and I didn't even know which way to go to the taxi stand.

An overpowering feeling of being lost came over me right then and there, and although I really had no reason to be worried or unhappy, I felt like bursting into tears. Maybe I had hoped against hope that Julian would appear at the railroad station despite his limp, being all loyal and brave, one hand resting on his crutches, the other hand holding the bouquet of roses I had dreamed of.

Screw it. That's a stupid, cheesy thought if there ever was one. I scolded myself for being so sentimental and started walking. I went through the pedestrian underpass and turned left, toward the neon lights. The tiny railroad station looked crummy and smelled of cigarette smoke, the ticket counter seemed long abandoned, and the only sandwich place there was just closing, blinds clattering shut. Besides me, there were only two middle-aged women who stood in the open glass doors and seemed to be waiting for a ride. I stepped toward them, looking around. Faceless buildings lined the town square: bank, doctor's office, drugstore, everything looked the same, and everything looked closed. The only sign of life I found was at a fast-food stand where I spotted the pierced and tattooed couple again, feeding their cute little doggie a piece of sausage. I wondered if they put mustard on the sausage to make the dog hot? I sighed. Julian would have enjoyed this little wordplay. But Julian wasn't here, and I couldn't see any taxicabs anywhere. Maybe they were all out driving, maybe I just wasn't fast enough getting off the train, and maybe the handful of other travelers had snatched the last few taxis right from under my nose. Hesitantly, I approached the two women.

"Normally there are a several taxis here," one of them said.

"At this hour, Heidi?" queried the other one.

"I'm sure they only just left. Just wait here for a little while."

I put my hands in my pockets. The day had been sunny and warm, but now, in the evening, you could really feel that it was autumn.

The two women continued their conversation without taking any further notice of me.

"Ah, Irene wouldn't even notice if the girl didn't spend the night at home," one of them said to her friend, speaking in the local Rhenish dialect that was unfamiliar to me. "You know, this Alina girl has her own little space up in the converted attic. It's like a proper little apartment. She only ever comes down to drop off her dirty laundry or to get something to eat from the kitchen."

"Hah, that certainly has its advantages. I tell you, if we had enough space I would love to banish my Dustin to the attic or the basement, just so I wouldn't have to listen to his terrible music all day long."

The first one chuckled.

"Yeah, you're right, but you see how dangerous that can be, too. Just imagine if the girl hasn't been home since Tuesday night. What if something happened to her?"

"Let's hope not," the second woman replied and started to move. "There's Reiner."

A car entered the town square, and while both women were walking toward it, I heard the first one say, "Okay, but I can see where Irene is coming from. If I were her, I would have gone to the police, too."

The women got into the car and it left. No taxicab anywhere in sight. Several minutes passed; nothing happened.

I was cold. Should I get my big sweater from the backpack? And how long should I wait, anyway? What if there was no taxi at all? I paced up and down and tried to fight my mounting unease. Oh, how I wished that at least my cell phone worked! Maybe then I could have persuaded Julian to come and get me. Of course, I could always call a taxi from the fast-food stand. But how long would that take, and how much would it cost to order a taxi specially? I didn't have that much money, and what little I had I needed for the weekend ahead.

5

There was a map of the area attached to the wall next to the main entrance of the railroad station. While someone had recently spat against the Plexiglas window that covered the map and I kept a careful "yuck" distance, I was nevertheless able to make out the location of the railroad station, the town center, Mühlbach Creek, the hiking trail following the creek, and finally the Rauschenmühle water mill. If my calculations were right, the distance from the railroad station to the water mill could be no more than one and a quarter miles if you took the trail along the creek. The actual road was much longer. This was because it made quite a detour from the railroad station and town center. The forest was a nature conservation area and only non-asphalt forest roads were allowed, with the Rauschenmühle water mill of course located deep inside the forest. So it would have been silly to follow the main road; this would have taken me at least an hour. The hiking trail through the forest, therefore, seemed like the obvious choice. I couldn't really get lost because the trail followed the creek bed the entire time, and even if it really got pitch dark under the trees I should still be able to hear the rushing water. I stared at the map hesitantly. Should I risk it? I glanced across the town square one last time. That must be the bridge crossing Munkelbach Creek over there. I saw the pierced/tattooed couple again, on their way, dog trotting behind. How I would love to follow and even join them! Anything not to be alone anymore! This was depressing; this was getting me down!

I had a lump in my throat, and I felt it getting bigger the longer I stood there. I swallowed hard. Just don't start panicking now! What had I been going over with the fox guy, over and over again? "Don't let your fear paralyze you; get moving, and something will move inside of you!"

Wasn't it better to start walking no matter what than to stand here as if all dressed up with nowhere to go?

Of course, a big, dark, unknown forest was not really my thing, but I really couldn't wait any longer. It was unbearable.

Cautiously, I started walking. Oh yes, that *was* better. With every step I took, I felt the strain that was choking me fall away.

I crossed the bridge. Munkelbach Creek had become a gushing, gurgling little river after all the summer rain. The hiking trail was impossible to miss, and in a minute, I would put on my sneakers to cope with any tree roots and bumpy patches. These thoughts helped calm my nerves a little. I was well prepared, even if my cell phone no longer worked.

After the bridge, I took a left turn onto a slow-traffic, residential road. The cobblestones were covered in warm, cozy light coming from the streetlights. Geraniums were in full bloom in front of brightly lit windows; you could hear the clattering of pots and pans, and sounds coming from TV sets. I grabbed the straps on my backpack, pulled my arms tighter to my side, and continued quickly. There would be no taxicab making its way to the railroad station

in this backwater town anyway, and I also wanted to prove
something to myself with this little hike—that is, that I
wasn't afraid, not of people and not of a big dark forest,
either. Taking this trail would put me to the test, a test that
I wanted to pass with flying colors. I wanted the fox guy to
be proud of me, and Julian would shake his head but then
he would kiss me and say, "I knew it! You're always full of
surprises!"

At that moment, I heard an engine running behind me
and turned around: a taxicab. It crossed the bridge, made
a U-turn on the town square, and parked right at the taxi
stand in front of the fast-food place. I mulled this over.
Should I go back and get in? That's what any sensible young
woman would have done. But I had never been one, and I
didn't. No, I wouldn't cop out now.

After about a quarter mile, the road made a fork. The
asphalt part of the road, which was lined by little single-
family homes, took a sharp right turn away from the creek
and up the hill. The other part, which was running parallel
to the creek, was marked as a dead-end road and only paved
with cobblestones. There were fewer houses, and they were
framed by bigger yards and gardens. I paused for a moment
and changed my shoes, wanting to be as quiet and nimble
as the white-socked tabby cat that was just crossing the road
in front of me.

I encountered no one. The houses farthest out were surrounded by high hedges and stood so far back that I could
barely even see the lights coming from their windows. I reached the end of the dead-end street and, standing under
the very last street light, started to realize just *how* dark it
was. Earlier, on the well-lit town square, it didn't seem that

dark to me *at all*. And while I had overheard the conversation of the two women, I hadn't really taken it in. Only
now did I realize that this casually uttered sentence about
the missing girl—what was her name again, something with
an A—seemed like a very significant piece of information,
a cautionary tale stressing the dangers of the forest, of the
dark. I felt myself starting to shake. Why exactly hadn't I
gone back to the taxi stand and gotten into that cab? Most
likely it was no longer there, probably carrying new passengers or driving around looking for a new fare.

The trail began right in front of my feet, first mean-
dering through a wild meadow for a few yards, only to
disappear behind a wooden bridge crossing the creek and
underneath the pitch-black canopy of trees. A big wooden
sign sporting a stylized squirrel was attached to the lamppost
and announced that I was now on the *Romantic Munkelbach
Valley Circuit Trail*. The squirrel was amateurishly carved
and seemed more voracious than cute to me. Also, the
timelines indicated underneath the writing—especially the
first, *Rauschenmühle water mill, 30 minutes*—were not very
encouraging, although I told myself that this was aimed at
casual day-trippers and slow-walking senior citizens, not at
teens such as me. *I* could walk so much faster. Despite my
heavy backpack, I hoped.

Before I started out, I looked at my wristwatch again, held
it right up to the streetlight so that I could see the clock face:
eight o'clock! Didn't seem like nighttime to me. It wouldn't
even be nighttime for another thirty minutes. People took
their dogs for walks at this hour. So why shouldn't I be bold
and unafraid and walk along this romantic trail toward my
beloved Julian?

The trail was almost impossible to miss, just as I had thought, even deep inside the woods. My eyes quickly adapted to the darkness, a little moonlight came through the canopy, and the creek murmured tirelessly to my right. And yet it took less than three minutes for me to stumble and fall for the first time. While I was massaging my sore knee, I tried to listen to all the sounds around me. The burbling creek drowned out many of them, though not the husky call of the screech owl over on the other shore, or the rustling of dead leaves directly behind me. Probably an acorn that just fell down, or a mouse. "Definitely not the infamous Munkelbach killer squirrel, Eva," I told myself aloud, laughing at my own joke and forcing myself to keep going.

I was walking too fast, too hastily. I could feel it by the thin film of sweat soon running down my back. Also, this trekking backpack was heavier than I had thought and my shoulders started aching. But I didn't want to stall! I wanted to get to Julian, and I wanted to get out of these woods.

Here we go! A suspicious crackle coming from the undergrowth, a feeling that someone was following me? All inside my head! There was nobody here but me.

"Are you afraid right now?" the fox guy had once asked me during one of our sessions when our conversation had turned to something extremely unpleasant and I had to hold onto my knees because they were shaking so badly. I hadn't given him an answer; instead, I hoped that he hadn't noticed, which of course was a delusion since he monitored every single one of my movements constantly. It wasn't just a coincidence that his name was Dr. Fuchs—"Fuchs," aka the fox; he also showed all the typical characteristics foxes were said to possess. He was clever, cunning—sly as a fox, so to speak—and seemed terrifying to a wuss such as myself, even though his face could be gentle and friendly at times.

"Why?" he had asked, and stretched the word out deliberately. "What do you think might happen?"

"Nothing, nothing at all," was the right answer. "Mice, owls, and squirrels won't hurt me! And besides, I'm not scared."

And so I continued, with every step trying to get used to the voices of the forest and, after a little while, even keeping a curious eye out for that owl whose calls I kept hearing. I felt strong until I reached an intersection where my trail crossed the forest road.

At first, it was just a matter of spatial orientation. I hadn't noticed this intersection on the area map by the railroad station; maybe it was an older map and the wide, graveled forest road hadn't been marked on it yet. It came from the left and down the hill, led across a bridge made of wooden planks over to the other side of the creek, and then followed, as far as I could see, the creek bed. Was this the trail I was supposed to take? The Rauschenmühle water mill, where Julian was waiting for me, was on this side of the creek. But the hiking trail seemed to have stopped. Could it be that it had become overgrown over time because everyone now used the forest road instead? Or did the old trail start farther up or farther down, maybe right where the bridge spanned the creek? I hesitated, and then took cover inside a wooden rain shelter, unloading my backpack onto a bench that was provided for tired and hungry hikers—from which it promptly plopped down with a muffled sound. I left it there and briefly relaxed my strained shoulders.

I heard the car engine just as I decided to start looking for the start of the trail farther down. In a matter of moments, the backpack and I disappeared underneath the bench, and the car roared across the bridge. Gravel crunched and brakes screeched as the off-road vehicle came to a stop in front of the rain shelter. Engine off, silence; and in it, the muffled drone of a stereo, my pounding heart, and my heavy breathing that was way too loud.

I'd had nightmares about such situations a million times before.

Calm down, Eva, don't think, don't move, don't breathe.

Doors opened. The music became deafeningly loud at first, then was dialed down and replaced by a voice: "Okay asshole, you can walk from here!"

Somebody fell from the car and landed with a thud. A person who was no longer struggling. He or she lay there, body contorted, and didn't move. Next, a young male got out of the car, kicked the person lying on the ground, stood there, put his hands on his hips, and started looking around.

I squeezed my eyes shut and made myself as small as possible under that bench. Whatever it was that was going on here, it probably wasn't very healthy to witness it all.

"So what should we do with him now?" an aggressive voice asked, and although I was shaking all over and thinking that I would start screaming at any moment, I opened my eyes again. The other passengers in the off-road vehicle—three young males and a female with long, ash-blonde hair, wearing boots and miniskirt—formed a circle around the person lying on the ground. A lighter blazed up, lit their faces for a few seconds.

"Wow, that went totally wrong," the girl shrieked. "Can't you just search him one more time? Maybe he *does* have it on him!"

"Do it yourself. I'm not touching him again!" One of the young males—they couldn't be much older than myself—left the group and, to my horror, started moving toward the rain shelter. My heart began to race; the ground I was lying on seemed to give way as if it, too, was trying to pull away from danger. But the young male didn't seem to notice me. He turned around again, stopped, and leaned against one of the supporting pillars of the shelter with his back to me. He stood so close that I could smell the smoke of his cigarette and read the white lettering on his windbreaker, reflecting in the moonlight: *Munkelbach 79 Sports & Athletics Club—Team Handball.*

"I won't touch him, either! He stinks." A second boy separated from the group and sat down on a pile of logs that was illuminated by the car's headlights. "Goddammit, this really sucks!"

"Not only does he stink like a pig, he is one, too," affirmed the third boy, who was still standing by the car. "First he runs his mouth and provokes people, and then he pees his pants. Love it."

"He's so gross," the girl said, talking herself into a rage. "I always hated him, even in first grade when he always ran after us and was being such a smartass, stupid nerd!" She kicked the victim, who didn't move, didn't even moan.

"Pipe down, Laura!" called the first boy, who was standing nearest to me. "Enough is enough."

"Enough, you say?" the third guy barked at him. "Dude, have you got Alzheimer's? Enough is never enough for this guy. Let's recount the facts: We don't have the cell phone. We have no access to his computer. We don't know if he's been printing more photos in the meantime or if he maybe even sent them out all over the Internet. He screwed us this way and that, and next thing you know he'll run to Daddy and tell on us—like, that we've been messing him up. He can take a lot more, if you ask me!"

"I'm all for it," said the second guy, who grabbed a big branch, lifted it up in the headlights as if to check its suitability, mumbling, "Almost as good as a baseball bat," and returned to his victim.

Other people would have interfered at this point, would have come out from under that bench, would have exposed the attackers as the mean, cowardly jerks that they were, and would have rushed to the victim's help without any regard for their own safety. Other people—that is, people of strong character, brave conflict mediators, and karate-fighting heroes—not me.

I shrank deeper down under that bench as if I was the one about to be beaten up. I shut my eyes and ears, I clenched my teeth because I thought I would throw up at any moment, and when vertigo announced itself I allowed it to come, grateful that it carried me away from this place and all my senses with it. It only subsided when the sound of the car's starting engine got through to my ears. So they were leaving. This was my cue: I could return to my body. I was again able to feel the little pebbles that were poking me in the back, the stale taste in my mouth, and the film of sweat on my skin. I had no idea how much time had passed, but I was still in the forest, and I was still alive. That, at least, was something. Very carefully, I opened my eyes.

The victim was lying in the same spot, motionless, still in the same contorted position. Only one of the perpetrators remained outside, legs apart, hands on his pants, and upper body bent back at the waist—as if he wanted to pee on the lifeless figure on the ground.

"Don't!" the car's driver snapped at him—this must be the boy who had stood next to me. "Enough! We're not going down to that level!"

"Hey dude, I was only kidding." The boy snorted noisily, spat, walked around the car, and got in.

Before they left, the driver leaned out of the window— he was looking in my direction, did he really not see me?— and said in a loud voice, "Maybe I'll come back in an hour or so, to see if you actually managed to get up and walk home. I mean, we're no monsters, right?"

The driver cranked up the engine, someone turned the music back on—hard, droning basses that made the forest vibrate and scared off any and all wildlife—the car backed up a little, turned, steered across the bridge, and drove off on the other side of the creek.

The boy they had called a nerd and a pig didn't make a sound. He just lay there where he was and didn't move.

I did the same.

6

I can't remember with certainty how much time had passed. I remember the damp cold rising from the forest floor and up my back, and the pale moon. I wished I were lying in my bed, just waking up from a nightmare, and my greatest fear was to fall asleep again and be part of the sequel. But this ill-fated day was not a nightmare, and the returning sounds of nature appealed to my reason. I mustn't close my eyes, and I mustn't fall asleep; I would freeze to death out here on this early October night.

I looked over to the boy. Precisely at that moment, the narrow silhouette of a fox passed him at a safe distance. It stopped, silently sniffed the air, and cantered off in a straight line, unfazed. I suddenly had a horrible thought: What if the boy was dead? What if the fox had smelled that this human being was no longer danger- ous, and what if that was the only reason it had come so close?

I worked up all my courage and crawled as silently as I possibly could from under the bench. The backpack was in the way, it made a scraping sound as I pushed it across the gravel. When I pulled myself up on the wooden bench, a splinter dug into my hand. I felt pins and needles in my left leg; I could barely put any weight on it, but I needed to now. I really had to start taking action.

I went over to the boy lying on the ground, weakly dragging my backpack behind me. He was lying on his side with his back turned to me, his arms pulled up to his face.

"Hello?" I said, and the sound of my frail, high-pitched voice startled me. I also had the feeling that the entire forest would now listen to what I was going to say and do next. It wouldn't be much. I had never attended a first-aid class, and I would definitely try to run if the boys in the off-road vehicle were to come back.

"Can you hear me?" I bent down to the boy and reluctantly felt the light-colored, well-insulated sports jacket he was wearing. I was going about it so cautiously that I barely even touched the fabric. And yet, he winced.

"Can I do something? Are you in pain? Do you want me to help you up? I—" I have no idea what to do in this type of situation, is what I wanted to say. But I couldn't utter the words. I squatted down next to him, trembling, and awkwardly caressed his head with my hand. In so doing, I recorded all the details as if they were happening to someone else and had nothing to do with me. I noticed his distinctive smell, saw his sweaty hair, his swollen eyes, the laceration on his upper lip. Next to him lay the branch one of the perpetrators had threatened and probably beaten him with. A little farther away, I saw the dirty baseball cap they must have taken from him and that their car had then run over.

I could hear his very short, very quick breaths.

Suddenly, I knew that he was afraid of me.

"Hey, it's okay," I said soothingly, but he seemed to think that I was that blonde girl. He crawled away from me in a desperate effort and held his arms—his jacket was torn at the elbows—protectively over his head.

"My dad has the cell phone," he yelled. "There's nothing I can do; I can't get ahold of the photos!"

"I don't care about that. I'm not one of them. I just came by accidentally."

The boy moaned quietly. Maybe he was crying?

"You don't need to be scared anymore, they're gone. But you can't stay here. Try to get up. Come on, I'll help you." I touched him again. He recoiled, letting out a sound that reminded me more of a cat being hit by a car than of a human being. I felt shaken and helpless, and I called out, "It's too cold to be lying here. Besides, they might come back. Please, please, let me help you!"

"I don't need any help!"

"Do you think you can get up?" I tried again to offer my hand.

"Let go of me! Leave me alone, all of you!" He doubled up in pain, wept. "I can manage by myself, like it matters anyway. Go! Please, go!"

He won't manage by himself, I thought. He hasn't even figured out that I'm not one of his attackers. Maybe he couldn't even walk by himself, probably had internal injuries, would freeze to death.

"I'll run over to the mill, and from there I can call for help: paramedics, police, your parents…" I didn't know his name, but that was something I wouldn't find out now anyway.

"Go!" The boy almost begged me. He was in shock. I had to hurry.

I grabbed my backpack. In my hurry to pull it up from the ground I got it the wrong way round, turned it over awkwardly, heaved it onto my exhausted shoulders.

"I'll be as quick as I can. I promise!" I repeated the last two words more to reassure myself. "I promise, I promise," I said while searching for the start of the trail, frantically running up and down, finally finding it after a few minutes, and, panting, looked over one more time at the sobbing heap of a person on the ground.

"I'm getting help! I will bring my boyfriend. I'll be right back." With a few quick steps, I stumbled into the forest.

The mill was still a good distance away. Soon I was soaked in sweat again and wheezing from physical effort; a little while later, I also had a headache because in my panicked hurry I had collided with a low-hanging tree branch. This part of the trail was less well traveled than the first section. Also, it ran well over three hundred feet above the creek bed, along the hillside, making the creek very difficult to hear. Somewhere along the line I stopped because I thought that, to top it all off, I had gotten lost. I stood there, ribcage heaving and head bursting with a headache, surrounded by thorny shrubs, and felt like bursting into tears.

But then I finally spotted the life-saving light in the distance. The Rauschenmühle water mill looked heaven-sent and unearthly to me: A place that offered me a level of protection I had only experienced in the fox guy's office up until now. A place where I would find help for that badly beaten boy. A place where someone was longingly, lovingly waiting for me.

7

Julian was sitting on the brightly lit courtyard patio—bandaged foot elevated—from which he was able to keep an eye on the hiking trail, the bridge across the creek, and on the access road. The mill itself, made of quarry-stones, was in the shape of an L and was overgrown with wild vines. Bright auburn leaves gleamed warmly and welcoming. I had arrived! I was safe!

When my boyfriend saw me, he got up from his garden chair with a start and limped toward me. "Finally! I was beginning to worry!"

"Julian!" I ran toward him and threw myself into his arms with such force that I nearly knocked him over.

"Eva, where have you been for so long? And look at you!"

Being close to him was so comfortable, so soothing, that I immediately started to cry.

"Something happened in the forest—"

"In the forest?" He let go of me. "Why didn't you take a taxi at the railroad station?"

"There were no taxis!" I cried all of my stress and tension out into the world. "I did wait, but no taxi came, and so I hiked through the forest, and then…"

"But I told you that you shouldn't—"

"I know," I sobbed, "but..."

"Okay, okay, it's alright, what's done is done." Julian lifted his hands in appeasement and quickly looked around, as if he was trying to figure out what we could or should do next. "Let's go inside!"

But I had already shed my backpack and slumped down into the second garden chair, exhausted. "I have to go back," I said with a sniffle and poured myself a good amount of tea from the thermos—which stood on the table—into Julian's cup. It was steaming hot, well-sugared Rooibos, and it burned my tongue.

"You're going to do *what*?" Julian asked in disbelief and reluctantly sat down in the other chair.

"I have to go back into the woods! There is a boy who's been beaten up pretty bad. By four teenagers in an off-roader. I saw the whole thing. Those were real *thugs*. There was a girl with them, too, and they—"

"Oh shit!" Julian exclaimed and grabbed his forehead.

"Yes," I yowled, lowering my eyes and holding onto the tea mug with both my hands. "I was terrified that they would hurt me, too, but they never saw me."

"Great! Thank God you're okay." Julian seemed relieved, but also confused and preoccupied. "Lower your voice, Eva! This boy—did he see you?"

"Yes, of course, I went over to him. I told him that I would get the police or the paramedics..."

Julian opened his eyes wide and grabbed my hands, pressed them against the warm tea mug. I thought he was encouraging me to keep on talking and quickly gave an account of the whole situation.

My boyfriend listened to me, visibly shocked. He then took a deep breath, peered to the left and right as if to make sure that nobody was listening, pushed the mug aside, placed my hands—still warm from the hot tea—to the cool back of his neck while leaning so far across the table that our faces almost touched, and said quietly and urgently, "That was a real bad situation for you, and I'm sorry. But still: Don't panic! If this guy doesn't want any help, then he's not going to need any, either. It probably looked a lot worse than it was. I don't think it's necessary to always get involved in everything. You're all wound up, Evie, and so am I. You know, I got a good fright myself. But I think we shouldn't be too obsessed over it. If we call the cops, that would probably be overreacting. No, no, wait! Don't start screaming again. Listen to me: I'm sure that it was just some super-intense disagreement between teenagers. You know, some type of a schoolyard brawl—horrifying to watch from the outside, but looking much worse than it actually was. Jeez, maybe this guy stole somebody's girlfriend!" He forced himself to smile, kissed away my tears—though not very successfully, as they just kept on coming.

Tenderly, he added, "You were all alone in a deep, dark forest; you didn't know your way around; you didn't know what it was all about; it seemed much worse to you than it actually was. It's understandable."

Julian probably just wanted to comfort me with such words; he probably said them with the best of intentions to help and console me, but I felt like I was being patronized.

Of course, I thought defiantly, *that's* how it must have happened! I was overreacting as usual, and Julian was right: That boy had just been teased a little. He's not lying badly hurt in the forest, he's putting on a show because he's a sissy who starts crying every time somebody steals his favorite baseball cap. He's a wuss like me who makes a mountain out of every molehill and suspects every stranger of being a possible threat. I withdrew my hands from his. He noticed how angry I was and backed down.

"I wasn't there, Evie, I have no way to judge, but just think for a second: if he sent you away, if he asked you to leave, then he was probably embarrassed about the whole thing. We will, of course, do what you think is right. But do you really think you're helping him if you turn this into a big deal and get the cops to take him home? Maybe he wants to take care of whatever this is himself."

I hesitated. These arguments made a little more sense to me. I, too, preferred to keep issues to myself and didn't appreciate my parents commenting on absolutely every single little thing. When I call them later to tell them that I've arrived, I won't tell them about my adventures in the forest—because it's pretty obvious what they would say.

"He's probably not even there anymore. I'm sure he wasn't all covered in blood and lying there half-dead, was he?"

"No," I had to admit.

"Did he have any broken bones? Was he groaning with pain? Did they take away his clothes, his money, his cell phone?"

"There *was* something about a cell phone!"

Julian bit his lip and turned his head to the side. "Evie," he said with great control, "all I want to know from you is if *you* think that we need to get involved. If I could walk, I would just go into the woods myself and take a look. But I can't walk; you know that. And I certainly won't allow you to go again by yourself. Anyway, I'm mad at myself for not ordering a taxi from here and having it pick you up at the station."

"Please don't be mad," I said in a flat voice. "I'm okay. I just got a little scared."

Julian was silent.

I took a sip from my teacup. The feeling of hot tea in my mouth restored my sense of normality. Here I was, alive and drinking tea. I remembered a few relaxation techniques the fox guy had taught me, and I was able to apply them. I focused on my body and returned to my center, taking small, deliberate mouthfuls of tea in between slower and slower breaths. Now it was time to make a decision.

"Ask your inner self," the fox guy would say while putting a hand on his stomach. "Listen to your inner voice. How do you feel right at this moment? And what is the first thing you would do if you were alone?" And although in principle I thought it was silly, I followed his advice and closed my eyes.

"Oh, come on, Eva," Julian said impatiently. "Don't be sitting there like my granddad when he doesn't want to listen and pretends to have chest pains. Let's go inside, please, and forget about this whole thing. I'm sure it wasn't that bad."

"But it was that bad!" The words burst out of me like an explosion.

"But it's none of your business!" Julian got louder, too, and bumped against the table so that the cup fell down and shattered on the tiled floor.

It was at that moment that I saw the man.

He had his hands on his hips and stood, half-hidden, on the neighboring patio behind a screen made up of a long row of potted plants. And even though I couldn't see the expression on his face because it was in the shadows, my immediate thought was that he had been following our conversation.

"Julian, someone is listening," I whispered, terrified, and reached for the pieces of the broken cup.

Julian bent down, too, but he didn't collect the pieces of ceramic. Instead, he lifted them from my fingers and hissed at me with such urgency that I didn't dare to object: "Leave it, we'll do it tomorrow. We're going inside right now. We should have done that earlier. Now go, and don't mention that fight again!" He took my hand and pulled me—quickly, despite his injured foot—into the house.

The man remained outside without saying a word.

"Who was that?" I asked as soon as we were inside.

"Our landlord," Julian answered brusquely.

"Why does he have such an evil look on his face?"

"Because he's an idiot!" Julian hissed. He turned off the outside lights, remembered that we could be seen much better in the well-lit interior that way, and angrily turned the outside lights back on. The man was gone.

"There, it worked. He can go complain to my dad if he wants to! I don't know what he could possibly accuse me of! I was just sitting here, all quiet and all, and I wasn't even playing music."

"He's been listening to us the whole, entire time. Maybe he'll call the police and file charges against us. Isn't there 'duty to rescue'?"

"He doesn't even know who we were talking about!" Julian yelled.

"But we don't know either!"

"No, of course not." Julian's face turned crimson. He turned around in furious anger and went into the kitchen. There—I followed him—he poured himself a glass of wine, leaned against the oven, stared at his feet, and tightened his fist around the wineglass with such strength that I was afraid he would break it.

"I'm sorry that all this happened," I whispered, almost crying again. "I definitely don't want to fight. I was so looking forward to our weekend."

Julian let out a puff of frustration, thought better of it, put down his wineglass, and held out his arms. "Me too," he said.

I cuddled up to him. At that moment, we heard an engine starting outside. We looked out the window that was facing the alleyway between the mill's living and working quarters. A jeep with the headlights turned on was just backing out of the part that must have been the former gear house. Out there, the driver—it was the landlord—got out of the car one more time, walked over to the building wall, took a long object that was leaning against it, and shouldered it. Before he left, he shot us a glance through the kitchen window. Then he roared off.

"Would you look at that, our friend Bernd here is going deer hunting again. Jeez, must give him a great deal of satisfaction, seeing how frustrated he is otherwise!"

I didn't immediately get what Julian meant by that, but I didn't need to ask because he promptly explained: "Bernd Vollmer, the landlord, he owns the mill. He lives next door."

Julian pointed with his head back toward the house. "He's been single for years. He's always putting on a show as if he's your best buddy and such a nature lover and keeps on saying how he doesn't hunt anymore. But I'm guessing he has loads of little secret, sadistic hobbies."

"What?"

"Oh, forget it. He's just this really annoying guy." Julian tried to play it down. "He's a know-it-all and very nosy. He's always checking if you forgot to turn all the lights off before you left the house, or if you're going too fast on a road you're not supposed to be on. He's a total pain, I tell you."

"But why did you rent your vacation home from him in the first place?"

"My parents get on well with him," Julian replied off-handedly, slipping from our embrace, turning back to his glass of wine, and pouring one for me as well. "Let's not talk about our stupid neighbors anymore," he said and, with a nod, invited me to take the second wineglass so we could raise our glasses together. "Let's forget Vollmer! Let's drink to our weekend!"

I didn't dare to tell my boyfriend that I didn't really drink and that I would rather have gone without since I was told to avoid alcohol, even though I had stopped taking regular medication ages ago.

Fortunately, the first mouthful didn't seem so bad. The taste of soft, ripe blackberries and chocolate only made my tongue feel furry and left a brief, warm sensation in my throat.

"An Australian Syrah." Julian swirled the wine in his glass, trying to sound sophisticated. "Daddy will have half a heart attack if he finds out that we peasants are guzzling his good stuff. But I needed something special to go with my first homemade pizza."

"Okay, but what are we going to do, Julian?" I asked with an impatient glance at the kitchen clock, which showed 8:51 p.m. "What if this man is now looking for that boy, and what if people later talk about us not helping…"

"Eva! How many times do I have to tell you: Bernd is going deer hunting! I'm sure he didn't hear everything; he couldn't have been standing on the patio all that long. I would have noticed, believe me!"

"Regardless, maybe we should do something, just in case." I realized how whiny I sounded. That was something I had really wanted to avoid, but my head was spinning from all these thoughts tumbling through my mind: What if that boy really was badly hurt? What if this Bernd Vollmer guy really came across him by accident and then made a connection between him and this agitated girl, i.e. me? Or what if Bernd Vollmer didn't find him because he went hunting elsewhere—I mean, what if no one found him and the poor guy froze to death out there? What if that boy was still hoping for that nameless girl to come back who had promised to help him! What if the perpetrators—or one of them, the most violent, the most hateful—came back instead!

"Jeez, I thought we had settled this!"

"No, we haven't, we were interrupted, and now so much time has passed, and—"

"Precisely," Julian said firmly. "If we wanted to intervene, we should have done so straightaway. But you weren't even sure yourself if we really needed to. Because the guy himself said that it wasn't necessary, and because in all *likelihood* it was only an alley fight like you see after any old football game. If it had been a car accident or a fistfight between stone-drunk hooligans, then I wouldn't hesitate for one second and would have used my cell phone."

I had to fight back my tears again. Julian treated me like a little child! And the really horrible thing about it was that the more we talked and the more time passed, the less sure I was of *how bad* my experience really had been.

Unfortunately, I couldn't deny that I get *very* frightened *very* easily. And even though I tried to keep this a secret from Julian, he seemed to instinctively feel that my judgment was not always quite what it should be.

"Believe me, Evie, you got a fright, and rightly so. But you're right to stay out of this. I mean, I think it's great how involved and helpful you are. You're a fantastic woman. I love you. But in this case, you're overreacting. That guy got back up on his feet and has gone home by now, trust me."

I nodded and ran both hands over my face.

"Yeah," I said. I was so tired, as if I hadn't slept in a week. "Whatever you say."

"Good." Julian seemed relieved. "How about you start by taking off your jacket? I should also take the pizza out of the oven; I'm afraid it got a little crispy."

He opened the oven door. Almost immediately, a delicious, promising smell filled the whole house.

Everything is normal, I told myself. We will eat pizza and enjoy our vacation. The scary part is over; the landlord is an idiot, but then again, most of them are; and the boy from the forest went home a long while ago—or over to his girlfriend's who will put an arm around his shoulders and talk to him in her sweetest voice: "I'm sorry that my ex is so jealous. Did you get hurt?"

I hoped I was right! Hopefully, Julian was able to assess the situation more accurately than I was! So why was I rejecting his help? Why was I having such doubts?

"We got lucky, nothing's burned. I can even leave it in the oven for a few more minutes. Come on, I'll carry your things upstairs and show you around. Do you want to take a shower—or eat first and then take a shower?"

I didn't plan to take a shower right after getting here, but because I was sweaty from walking and really needed to relax a little and because Julian was suggesting it, I thought it sounded like a good idea.

"I'll take a shower first."

"Okay." Julian beamed as if he preferred this response, too. He pressed his lips against mine and then stepped through the narrow hall—where I could see the actual front door leading out into the alleyway—back into the huge living room with the fireplace and the big plateglass windows that opened onto the courtyard patio. My backpack was still outside. While Julian was getting that and the thermos, I took a look around. The room was furnished with contemporary furniture, pop music was softly coming from the stereo, logs crackled in the fireplace, and the opposite wall sported Julian's three-year-old niece's first attempts at painting. There were children's paintings in the fox guy's office, too, fixed to the lilac wallpaper, which I always found very soothing.

"Pretty heavy!" Julian gave me a big grin, closed the door, and led the way, carrying my backpack into the hall and, at the end of the hall, up the spiral staircase. "Bathroom and bedrooms are upstairs."

I would have loved to say something, would have liked to share his joy in showing me around the cottage, but on the inside I was still too busy arriving.

"This is where we sleep. There—that's your wardrobe; I hope you have enough room. And here—this is the bathroom; you can use those towels over there. Down the hall is the second, smaller bedroom, but we won't be using it. Also, I didn't turn the heating on in there."

"Thanks."

"Now stop looking all freaked out. Take a nice long shower. I'll set the table in the meantime, and everything will be just fine."

"Alright. We'll just act as if nothing happened."

"Exactly." Julian massaged his bandaged foot.

I had forgotten all about his accident.

"Sheesh, what an idiot I am! I totally forgot to ask how *you're* doing in all this excitement!" I exclaimed and slapped my hand against my forehead.

"Don't worry." Julian gave me a meek smile. "It's sprained or something. I'll be okay. As long as you please chill out now."

We kissed. Then he gave me a little wave and slowly limped back down the staircase. I shouldn't have allowed him to carry my backpack, I thought, feeling a little guilty; his foot had seemed so much better in the kitchen earlier.

Okay, let's unpack quickly and get into the shower! I got undressed, opened my backpack, grabbed my toiletry bag, and reached for my journal. Yes, I know you don't need a journal to take a shower, but you do need it in moments like these—to lovingly press it against your chest, to feel and to prove how much you love yourself, to read about all the things you've experienced and scribbled down, to quickly add something, even if it was just one sentence: "Dear diary, I had a horrible, horrible evening, but I'm still alive!"

My hand grasped at—nothing.

My eyes grew very wide.

And before I realized what I was doing, I had started screaming.

The side pocket was almost completely torn off. Of its original contents—two apples, my journal, and my pencil case—only the pencil case was still there. It had slipped into the fold between upper and lower compartments and remained wedged in there. My journal and the apples had fallen out: on the train, by the railroad station, in the forest, somewhere, anywhere.

"Eva? What happened?" Julian was storming up the stairs.

"My journal is gone! Look! There's a big hole in my backpack!"

"Jeez! That's what all the screaming is about? And I thought you saw a burglar, or there's a fire, or you're in pain, or—" Julian shook his head. "A diary! Is it that important? I always thought that was something for little girls."

"It's important to me!"

My boyfriend rolled his eyes. "Okay, fine, we'll walk up the trail tomorrow and see if we can find it. Unless you lost it on the train."

"I think I still had it on the train. I...I don't know, I'm scared that...that..." My heart was beating so fast that it hurt. I couldn't speak.

"Eva." Julian squatted down beside me on the floor, took me in his arms. "You're completely rattled. Why don't you go take your shower. I will take a look and see if I can find your diary. Maybe it's in the living room or on the patio."

It wasn't there. I would have seen it.

"Evie, please," he begged helplessly, "please don't cry again. What kind of a weekend would that be, and the pizza's getting cold, too."

Don't you have a crying fit. Don't you even start. If you allow only one tear, so many more will come.

With great effort, I mumbled the word "shower" and felt my way into the bathroom. Only when I was finally in the shower, leaning wearily against the tiled walls and feeling the hot water drumming on my head—only then did I allow myself to cry.

8

My journal had been my comfort, my secret retreat, the pillow for my soul. Every time I experienced something exciting, every time I was full of love, fear, shame, or anger, and of course every time I came back from the fox guy—the first thing I always did when I got home was to spend time with my journal. Not only did I use it to describe all my tingling feelings for Julian in great detail, but I also wrote down and processed all my worst experiences, the ones that were more than just a little embarrassing. My journal reflected how miserable I had been before the move, to what extent my former classmates had tormented me in that youth hostel, what horrid nightmares I kept having, how many times I had been so scared that I barely managed to get onto the school bus in the morning, how I had isolated myself more and more, and how I had believed that *everyone* would notice my weakness and my inadequacies, and how they would turn away—sniggering or shaking their heads or being embarrassed.

My journal described that I was taking medication for dizzy spells and—last but not least—that I went to see a psychotherapist once a week. I knew, of course, that this was no reason to be ashamed. After all, you wouldn't be ashamed if you had a cavity and went to see a dentist, would you? My parents had used this argument a million times to try to reassure me. Still, they thought it was better not to tell the entire extended family: no need to rub it into everyone's face. That was why I hadn't told anyone up until now, except Sarah and my grandma.

Grandma immediately tried to trivialize my problems. "Why, you don't even need this, Evie," she had said, full of compassion, and I had felt even more stupid and inadequate because it was *precisely* what I needed.

Even my dad, who was much younger, of course, and lived his life with both feet firmly on the ground, had a hard time accepting it. He always tried to get around certain wordings. For example, he would never use the word "psychotherapist"; couldn't even say "Dr. Fuchs." The best he was able to come up with was saying something like, "Do you have an appointment with *that guy in the city* this afternoon?" And the one time he really had to go with me, he just sat there extremely tense and nervous and let my mom do most of the talking, even though he was never normally at a loss for words—quite the opposite, in fact.

Only Sarah was relaxed about it, thought that my family was behaving very oddly, and encouraged me all the time to talk about it with Julian. "How many anorexic girls are out there?" she liked to ask. "Do you really think they are all ashamed of themselves?"

But even though her constant support gave me courage, and even though I was becoming more self-confident and had already decided to let Julian in on it this weekend—I couldn't bear the idea that somebody might be reading my journal.

I had to prevent this at all costs!

I dried off quickly without blow-drying my hair; I just slipped into my clothes and went down the spiral staircase. The dining table in the living room was set but Julian wasn't there, nor was he in the kitchen. "Julian?" I opened the patio door.

"Hello?" No answer. The entire property lay still. I could only hear the splashing of the creek. Because it was so much darker here than in the city, I preferred to go right back inside. Once more, I searched the entire cottage. Where was Julian? He couldn't have disappeared into thin air! Maybe he had gone to look for my journal. Or maybe he was having second thoughts about that boy and was on his way to help him, in spite of everything. But he couldn't even walk properly!

I opened the front door leading out into the alleyway, just to do something, anything. After all, it was possible that Julian had gone to check that faulty patch up on the shed roof. Very carefully, I ventured outside. The gear house, where the jeep was parked, towered dark above me. How sinister that windowless building with its black slate roof looked! The small shed Julian must have been talking about was right next to it, on the left side. I walked a few steps, shivering and with my arms wrapped around my body. Julian was nowhere to be seen. Also, the roof looked pretty new to me—maybe he was talking about another shed?

"Sheesh, Julian, come on, where the heck are you?" I quietly moaned to myself and kept wiping tears off my cheeks. I would get a headache, too, and I wasn't even sure if I had packed aspirin.

Somebody was laughing. Quietly, muffled.

Was that the neighbor? Had he, while I was taking my shower, come back and was he now standing around the corner with a deer carcass on his back? Would he jump out in front of me, would he throw the dead animal—still warm—into my face, and would he reach for my throat?

No, no, no! I clasped my hands over my ears, as if I could shut out the voice of fear inside my head.

Laughter again. Julian's laughter.

"Julian!" I ran toward him as he was stepping from the garage door.

"Whoa!" he uttered in surprise. Something silvery fell from his hands, and he reached out his arm so that I wouldn't step on it in my nervous hurry.

"What are you doing out here?" he shouted, quickly picking up his cell phone from the ground and putting it into his jeans pocket.

"I was looking for you! I was scared!"

"Scared? Nonsense! Now seriously, pull yourself together!" He didn't give me a chance to hug him. Instead, he stormed into the house and pulled the pizza from the oven.

"Do we want to eat now or what?"

"But…"

For a moment we were silent—he, irritated; me, just about able to sit down in a chair. After two endless minutes, his face relaxed and he gave me a thin smile.

"I'm sorry. Do you think we can pull it together at some point this evening?"

"Maybe we should eat first," I suggested bravely, knowing full well that I really didn't feel like eating at all.

"Alright." Julian's smile turned into a stronger, more conciliatory smile. "I was in the garage checking my bike.

I thought you'd spend more time in the shower." He took a look at my wet hair.

I couldn't think of a single good answer. Asking him to come with me now and help me look for my journal seemed totally hopeless. It also seemed pointless to tell him about my psychological problems. Such thoughts were like a distant dream to me now. If I only hinted in that direction he would never take me seriously again.

"Don't you want to go dry your hair? Two more minutes won't matter. I don't want you to get sick just because you got here in such a hurry and don't feel comfortable here with me."

"I didn't say that I didn't feel comfortable here with you."

Julian nodded. "I know, but…maybe I overreacted a little bit. So if you want to go blow-dry your hair, go ahead— I'll stay right here and promise I won't go anywhere."

I would much rather go back into the woods to search for my journal, but I didn't feel strong enough to fight his gracious request, and so I smiled and got up. Whether or not I blow-dried my hair didn't matter. I did it because Julian asked me to, and when I was finished, I came back downstairs, got it together, and ate the slice of pizza he had put on my plate. I forced myself not to think about whether or not he had really checked his bike, or if he had maybe called somebody on his cell phone instead. But why should he do that? Send me into the shower just so he could call somebody in secret? We were freshly in love; we shouldn't be keeping *any* secrets from each other! But didn't I have my own little secrets, and didn't I feel ashamed of them myself, which kind of weakened my position? So I finished my plate like the good girl that I was and even had a glass of red wine to go with it. In the end, my head was spinning, but I said bravely, "It was delicious."

"Really?"

"Yes, really. I—" Whee-hee, how nice it was to be a little tipsy; at least my mind just went into suspended animation. "I mean, I'm so happy you made such an effort, and I'm really sorry I was such a party pooper today. But first I got such a fright in the forest, and then losing my journal…"

"Ah, the diary." Julian's facial expression turned into that kind, puzzled-amused look I liked so much on him and that I hadn't noticed all night. He put his hands on mine, raised his eyebrows, and said, "Okay, even though my foot needs some rest, you and I will get onto my bike right now and ride up that darn road all the way to the railroad station. At least the sections of the road I can safely ride on without breaking my neck. So, what do you say?"

"Oh Julian, you're the best!" I jumped up from my seat, knocked over my wineglass, and got onto his lap.

Everything would be alright! We would find my journal, would realize that the guy from the forest was gone and therefore obviously taken care of, and would—feeling relieved—return home. We would eat the rest of the pizza, snuggle up in front of the fireplace while almost falling asleep, and tomorrow we would laugh the whole thing off.

9

His motorcycle was a fairly new Enduro dirt bike with just
the right mix of shiny chrome and daredevil mud stains,
its engine sounding loud and aggressive, and when Julian
motioned for me to take a seat behind him, that overwhelm-
ing feeling of happiness I had felt earlier today returned. My
knight carried me on his steel horse away from this scary
place, he protected me with his strong arms, and he fixed
all of my problems. And when he took me home, heroic
deeds completed, I might allow him to carry me over the
threshold.

Even though the stuffy helmet on my head bothered
me—you couldn't really breathe in that thing, and the
thought of how many greasy-haired heads had used it
before me gave me a somewhat nauseous feeling—I smiled
blissfully as we left the mill's courtyard.

We didn't find my journal on the first part of the trail—
the section closest to the railroad station where I got lost
the first time—even though we both got off the bike and
searched to the left and right of the trail using our flashlights. And I very quickly realized that our search mission
was pretty hopeless, especially now, at night. After all, I had
charged through the brush earlier, panic-stricken, and had

gotten caught on thorny branches every six or seven feet. It could have fallen out *anywhere*.

"The old trail up to the rain shelter is way too overgrown. I won't ride on it in this darkness. Let's turn around and take the forest road instead." Julian got back on the bike, and I sat back down behind him without protest. He was right, of course; we shouldn't risk an accident for a missing journal. Besides, I was happy and proud about the efforts he made just to accommodate me. Not a word from him regarding his injured foot. My wish was his command, so to speak.

I held onto him tightly and relaxed into our speed as we thundered across the Mühlbach Creek bridge, along the graveled access road—more than one and a quarter miles long—that led us to the main country road, and from there, back to the forest road that would lead us to the creek in a wide arc. The darkness didn't scare me now. Here on the back seat, snuggling up to my boyfriend, I didn't care if the unearthly monsters of the night reached out to me with their long, thin, bony fingers—I was always faster; I was gone before they could grab me. I almost felt peace and serenity permeating my body; I didn't mind riding—riding fast—for hours. The more distance I put between myself and the mill, the better. I couldn't say what exactly my issue was with the water mill; there was no objective reason, aside from the fact that a landlord lived there who was shooting deer and whom Julian didn't like.

Only when Julian steered the Enduro dirt bike down into the valley and toward the rain shelter did my sense of calm suddenly dissipate.

Julian stopped. I yanked the helmet off my head. It was only then, in the bike's headlights, that I realized that the stretched-out, rigid form I had for just one second taken for the boy was really the long, horizontal shape of a log—the same log one of the perpetrators had sat on only two hours earlier.

I tried not to relive that scene in my mind's eye, tried not to have the rug pulled out from under me, tried to stay calm and reasonable.

"Was it here?" Julian didn't seem to notice my distress. "Well, at any rate, the guy is gone. What did I tell you, Evie—nothing bad happened here, it was just a bit of monkey business."

But didn't that one youth jump up, the one who was sitting right here, and didn't he raise a big branch above his head like a baseball bat? Did he bring it down in the end, or was he just faking it? I had closed my eyes right at that moment! Was it possible that I didn't witness the quarrel altogether correctly? There was no branch lying on the intersection that even looked like a baseball bat. Besides, I wouldn't have the strength to check if it had any blood on it. What for? So I could prove that I had assessed the situation correctly, that something more happened here? Besides, I needed all my strength just to keep my trembling under control, and I didn't want Julian to notice.

"Well, that's settled then." Julian turned on our flashlights, handed one to me. "Now all we need is your diary."

We walked up and down, searching, looking—that is to say, I staggered over to the rain shelter, knees unsteady, and looked under the bench. Julian briskly strode up and down the forest road; he probably wanted to get this over and done with as quickly as possible. Which was certainly understandable, because his foot was hurting. *Or was it?* I paused for a moment, observing him. The bandage hampered his movements, of course; he was a little wobbly and unsteady on his feet, but if his foot was hurting, then why did he put so much unnecessary weight on it to kick a pinecone out of the way?

"What is it? Did you find it?" Julian must have sensed me observing him, and turned around.

"No, unfortunately not," I replied and realized to my horror that he was now coming toward me, visibly limping again, as if caught red-handed.

"Then you must have lost it on the train." He stroked my arm with his hand—a tender, comforting, and at the same time immensely cautious and disassociated gesture. It wasn't something you would do if you were in love, and I didn't react like someone who was in love. I didn't take his hand, which was now hanging by his side, eight inches away from mine.

"Well, uh, what do you think? Should we go to the railroad station and take a look there?" Julian sounded a little unsure. He must have noticed my reluctance. He was probably feeling just as uneasy as I was. Maybe he also felt that we were on the verge of drifting apart, drifting away from each other, that a hairline crack had appeared in our love and that the smallest mistake would only deepen it.

"You probably want to go home," I whispered, and the thought crossed my mind that that's exactly where I wanted to go myself—home.

"No, no, my foot is much better. I sometimes even forget that I hurt it. I think I got lucky."

I nodded. So that explained why he had kicked that pinecone earlier. For the second time this evening, he gave me an explanation without my asking for it, and again it didn't quite convince me.

"Come on, Evie." He took my hand, now at least in the way a good friend would do. "Let's do it properly."

I climbed onto the dirt bike, forced my head into that horrible, anxiety- and asthma-triggering helmet, stiffly wrapped my arms around his body, and tried to remember that blissful feeling of happiness that I had only moments ago—gone!

Gone, just like my journal that wouldn't turn up: not on the hiking trail between rain shelter and town, not on the road leading toward the railroad station, not inside the railroad station or on the tracks.

Gone, just gone, exactly like my excitement about this vacation.

Half an hour later, we parked the bike next to Bernd Vollmer's jeep inside the garage and went into the living room without saying a word, cold leftover pizza still on the table. We cleared away the dishes, and as Julian reached for the bottle of wine, sighing, I went upstairs and put my clothes into the wardrobe. In doing so, I got ahold of my new nightgown. Vanessa and Vivien had helped pick it out, thought it was "insanely super-hot," and predicted that I would spend the hottest night of my life with him. Should I wear it? I would have to if I wanted to sleep tonight. I hadn't even packed my boring old pajamas. As soon as I put the negligee on, though, my endless disappointment gave way to a very empowering feeling of defiance: I might have issues, I might be a drama queen, but I certainly wasn't ugly.

Julian seemed to think so, too. I noticed how his eyebrows shot up—pleasantly surprised—when I came back into the living room. Unfortunately for him, though, he had already turned on the TV, emptied the bottle of wine, and, to top it all off, pointedly elevated his injured foot, which he had bandaged using an oversized ice bag—all in such a way that he appeared to be so seriously injured as to be completely immobilized. I went over to him and kissed him on the mouth. "I'm tired, I'm going to bed."

"I..." He opened his mouth, his eyes wandering from my eyes to my cleavage and back again; it was cute, spontaneously brave and shy/embarrassed all at the same time. Just like on that first day when we were waiting in line at the school snack store.

I knew of course that I still loved him. Also, I was sure that he felt the same way, in spite of it all, and that he would have preferred to clear up this bad vibe between us sooner rather than later. But something made him hesitate for just a split second, and that's when I turned around, said night-night, and went upstairs.

Right then and there I really wanted and needed my journal. But it was lying on the forest floor somewhere, and so I turned off the lights and curled up on the bed with my back turned toward the door and to Julian's side of the bed. I remembered that I had forgotten to call my parents. But if I called them now they would surely notice that I wasn't feeling well.

Julian came in twenty minutes later, tried his best to make just enough noise so that I would wake up but still think he was trying to be quiet, crawled in under the covers beside me, and wrapped his arm around my belly. I was happy, but I pretended to be asleep and not notice. In the end, it took me a long time to fall asleep, while Julian's regular breathing soon revealed that he was far out, drifting in his ocean of dreams. When I tried to relax, I had the feeling that the bed was turning or shaking as if during a minor earthquake. "Positional vertigo" is what it's called, and I tried to ignore it by focusing on every little creak and crack, on all the little sounds that were unfamiliar to me: wind, animal sounds, creaking floorboards, gurgling creek. When, in addition to all the eerie noise, today's images came flooding back into my head, I inched closer to my boyfriend.

18

Sunlight, burbling creek, the smell of coffee.

"Good morning, goodie bag!"

I opened my eyes. Julian had prepared a breakfast tray.

"Morning! Wow, this looks delicious! How nice!"

"I figured breakfast in bed would be just the thing."

"Yeah! And you even brought a little bunch of flowers!"

"Of course! The three roses are from by the shed wall, and the great big orange-colored ones I swiped from Vollmer's flowerbed. Thank God, that weirdo didn't see me. Or else he would be whining, 'Do you really think I'm growing them just for you? Don't you get a weekly allowance? I will tell your father! He needs to teach you some manners, or else there'll be a rent increase!'" Julian furiously wagged his finger in front of my face, kicking up such a fuss that I just had to laugh out loud. Not a moment later we were in each other's arms and kissing, relieved. What a difference a few hours of sleep and a little sunshine can make—suddenly everything seemed fine again!

Julian crawled under the covers and balanced the breakfast tray on our knees. As we were eating, we giggled and got closer. I kissed some breadcrumbs from the corners of his mouth; he braided a flower into my hair and was very adamant about fishing any fallen-off petals from between my breasts using his hands. No longer did we talk about the previous night; instead, we made plans for the day ahead. Julian wanted to show me the surroundings: the town, places of interest, the river. Maybe there would be time to meet his friends later on; since he'd been spending all of his vacations and most of his weekends here, Munkelbach was like a second home to him.

"It's gorgeous here, you'll see. Starting right now, you're going to love it." Julian put the tray with the leftover breakfast down on the floor and crawled back into bed, to me, so that we were facing one another. "And so that everything is perfect, Evie, I will go to the stationery store in a minute and get you a new diary."

"Oh, it's not that important," I muttered sheepishly. The racket I had caused over my journal now seemed over-the-top and childish.

"Oh, yes it is," he insisted. "I want to make up for your trouble. Because, you know, my foot feels fine again, and that's why I'm really blaming myself for not picking you up at the station. I was just feeling sorry for myself, while you were being super-strong and cool."

I felt myself blushing.

"Stop it!"

"But it's true!" He shifted closer and gave me a long and very passionate kiss. For a moment, I thought that *it* was about to happen—my first time—and how it was all moving a little too fast, despite the six weeks that Julian and I had officially been "together," despite last night when nothing happened, and despite that feeling of desire and anticipation and the fact that I was joyful and happy now, with everything between us finally back to normal. It really was, because Julian—who was just the perfect boyfriend—seemed to notice my hesitation and said, "I'm calling pillow fight, loser pays for ice cream!"

We both won, romped through the bed, chased each other down the stairs, out onto the patio and back up again, over the bed, and into the bathroom.

Half an hour later, I cheerfully stepped out onto the courtyard patio where Julian was waiting for me next to his dirt bike. The water mill now seemed so much friendlier to me. I was surprised to see that the grumpy landlord had shown quite a bit of talent when designing his side of the building: all of the window frames were alternately painted blue, yellow, and red; hand-carved stone and wooden sculptures were everywhere; a lazy cat was basking in the sun on the patio table; and deep inside the wild vine growing up the stone walls, I spotted not one but three chickadee nest boxes. Wow, I must have been a real mess last night! Just because it was dark and just because Julian mentioned that he didn't like him, I had been scared out of my mind of this man who lived in this cheerful little house. Typical! I always allow myself to be affected by other people's personal opinions and was unable to assess things realistically when in a stressful situation.

"You look fantastic!" Julian grabbed my hands and spun us around a few times, as if to dance. "Ready?"

"What about your foot?" I asked.

"All gone!"

"What do you mean, all gone?" I giggled. "Your entire foot is gone?"

"The pain is gone, smarty-pants!" He clapped his hands, rushed—still with a little limp—to get the doors locked, and motioned for me to get on the bike.

And we were off, first up the access road toward the main country road, and then, at a pretty good speed, down toward Munkelbach. Even the town itself seemed more inviting to me than last night. We ignored the newly constructed, dreary square in front of the railroad station and parked right in historic downtown, where the weekly farmers market was already in full swing. Julian bought a bag of grapes from one of the vendors, treated me to an expensive new diary notebook made of extra pretty paper, and insisted on picking out a bracelet for me in a jewelry store. Then we sat down by the bubbling fountain, gazed at the colorful facades on the traditional, half-timbered houses, and fed each other sweet grapes.

"Now, all I need is to start sending wish-you-were-here postcards."

Julian grinned from ear to ear.

"We can do that from the café. I owe you a big ice cream sundae anyway."

"Okay, but I'm paying this time."

"Why?"

"Because. Because you already spent enough money on me." I got up. Good for him that Julian always seemed to have enough money to throw around, but sometimes I just felt pretty poor, what with my regular weekly allowance and a dad who was an auto mechanic at a dealership garage instead of in some management position at a big power company.

"Alright." Julian took my hand. I was still holding a grape in one of my hands, and when we touched, it burst.

"Hey, whatcha doing?"

"Jelly! Do you want any?" He chuckled, put my hand to his mouth, and licked off the grape jelly sludge.

"You're an idiot," I said, brimming with happiness because he was nice and genuine, because of the sweet expression in his eyes, because he was now tickling my wrist with the tip of his tongue, because of this intense desire I felt for him—right now I really just wanted to get back to the mill and, in a mad rush, fall into bed together.

Maybe that would have been better for us. But we just had to have ice cream first, didn't we.

11

La Perla, the Italian ice cream parlor, was centrally located and bathed in sunshine. We ordered two cappuccinos and one *Coppa d'Amore* sundae for two. When Julian went to use the bathroom, I grabbed the *Munkelbach Gazette* someone had left on one of the neighboring tables. The report, showing a color photo of a girl, was the day's lead story and therefore impossible to miss.

Girl, 18, Missing Since Party

Eighteen-year-old Alina Westkamp, a Munkelbach native, went missing as long ago as late Tuesday night, October 2. The high school student attended a party with friends in the New High School auditorium, but apparently left unnoticed by her friends. Whether she went home alone or whether she had company is not known. Her parents didn't notice until early Wednesday evening that their daughter was not at home. Alina lives in the converted attic above the family home and is described as very independent. Initially, her parents assumed that she had left again to meet up with some friends. But when she was still missing after the second night, they contacted the police. With the help of the *Munkelbach Gazette,* the police are currently searching for the high school student and are asking readers who may have seen Alina either Tuesday evening or...

"Oh, you're reading that old rag? Anything interesting? You look totally absorbed."

"This girl…" I felt how I was breaking out in a sweat and slumped back in my chair. "Last night I overheard two women talking," I said to Julian. "I knew that a girl was missing, and what that could potentially mean. And still I went through that dark forest all by myself." The sheer realization of this made my heart beat faster. "I feel like I was tempting fate, like I ignored a big, important warning."

Julian looked at me with concern in his eyes.

"Calm down, Evie! You're okay; nothing happened."

"Still!" I was gasping for breath. How could I explain to Julian that I was scared—even though right here, sitting at a table in an ice cream parlor, there was no reason to be scared?

"Evie, what is it?"

I couldn't talk to him about my anxiety attacks, not here in public. I needed more quiet for that. And so I took a sip of my coffee, which had just arrived, listened to the Italian pop music coming from inside the café, and lied. "It's nothing. I'm fine, just low blood pressure." That was my parents' favorite explanation for my little *episodes*. Everyone is familiar with low blood pressure; it's an excuse that can be used for anything and everything, and it's almost always well received.

Julian nodded, but he seemed alarmed. Without taking his eyes off me, he asked, "Would you hand me the paper?"

That report had an effect on him, too. He stared at the girl's picture for a moment, opened his mouth, and started reading. He took no notice of the waiter who had just arrived with our sundae—adorned with little red paper hearts—nor of the two young males who stopped by our table right at that moment.

"Hey, look, it's Julian, and look how he's scarfing down that gigantic sundae!"

Julian cringed, and the two of them had a good laugh about their successful surprise attack. They amiably patted him on the shoulder and pulled up two chairs in order to sit with us, as if it was the most natural thing.

"Dustin," said one of them, extending his hand to me.

"Hi."

"And I'm Mickey."

"Eva." I couldn't manage more than a couple of one-syllable words, and Julian himself seemed a little irritated about the unexpected company. Reluctantly, he lowered the paper.

"Uh, yeah, hi, I already told you that my girlfriend was coming. Eva loves Munkelbach." He quickly looked at me and kissed me on the cheek.

The two youths—they were Julian's age and looked decidedly athletic—chuckled. It was clear that they took Munkelbach for a small backwater town that they want-ed to leave as quickly as possible after high school grad-uation. Dustin ordered a mug of coffee. Mickey snuck a sugar wafer from our sundae and, while munching, asked, "Heartbreaker? Hmm, are you a heartbreaker, Julian?"

"Shut up! Go order your own ice cream, and keep your stupid comments to yourself."

"Dude, I was just messing with you!" Mickey nudged Julian in the side and, using his teeth, snapped the rest of the sugar wafer in two. "And already I'm attracting negative attention, huh?" He grinned, leaned across the table, stared at me for a long time, and said, "Eva. So long awaited and so very longed for."

I didn't say anything. My pulse was still racing quite fast, I felt nauseous, and I didn't know what to make of these two. Their sudden appearance had made me even more nervous, but I couldn't say why.

"Did you read that thing about Alina?" Dustin asked next, accepting the coffee cup from the Italian waiter and eagerly taking a few sips.

"Just now," Julian replied and seemed as confused as I was.

"And? Do you think something happened to her?"

"No idea. You'd know better than I would." Julian looked at the paper. "I hope not, but I don't know her that well. I don't live here, remember."

Dustin shrugged his shoulders.

"When you live here, you don't know everything either. But Laura knows her well. She says that Alina often doesn't come home at night, that she once had a thing with a twenty-year-old when she was fourteen, even ran away with him and stuff. She said she wouldn't be surprised."

"Whatever. You can't trust a word Laura says. Every woman is a slut according to Laura, as long as she's better looking than her," Mickey erupted, leaning back in his chair and giving me a nod. "It's true. Don't be surprised if she's a bitch to you."

I guess that was supposed to be a compliment. In his eyes, I was better looking than a girl named Laura. *Laura*— I had heard that name last night. But of course, there were lots of girls named Laura.

"Doesn't matter what Laura says. But, you know, you gotta wonder," Dustin grumbled.

Mickey gave a wave of his hand.

"Enough already. You're scaring Julian's sweet little girl-friend, and she looks pretty pale already. By the way, what about tonight? Are you coming? We're celebrating. Emra's buying the first round. You're invited, too, Eva."

I think I was turning even more pale, but I got the feeling that Julian also felt uneasy about the invitation. He hesitated for a suspiciously long time.

"I thought your little plan wasn't going anywhere. We'll see. I don't know what our plans are yet."

"She's still buying drinks," Mickey countered, reaching over to Julian conspiratorially, covering his mouth with his hand, and cackling in a whisper: "What do you mean you have plans! Can't keep your hormones under control, dude, huh?"

I saw how annoyed Julian was. When Mickey reached for the second sugar wafer, Julian's face turned red. But he didn't object.

I was glad to see that Julian didn't enjoy this kind of joke and seemed to want to spend his vacation alone with me. And I wanted to back him up.

"Maybe another time," I said. "He sprained his ankle, and I only got here very late last night. All my trains were delayed, and then, when I was walking through the forest..."

But Julian interrupted me abruptly.

"Listen, Eva, I just remembered that you haven't called your parents yet. Do you maybe want to call them now? Here, you can use my cell phone." He handed me his phone and looked at me urgently.

Suddenly, I was scared. Had I said something wrong? Something to do with these boys? The way Dustin was sitting there, stocky, with his shoulders pulled forward, and the tone of voice in which Mickey had said "dude"—it all seemed painfully familiar.

Stop. Stop thinking right there! Julian had no way of knowing who was in the forest yesterday, and I myself didn't know, either. It had been dark, and there were probably lots of slim, athletic young males who knew girls named Laura. Just because these two had appeared out of nowhere, and just because Mickey had swiped two sugar wafers from us, this didn't automatically mean that they were bad guys. They were friends of Julian's. Friends of Julian's couldn't be thugs; it just wasn't like him.

"Go now," his eyes seemed to implore me.

Maybe I was just imagining things; maybe he only meant it just the way he said it, because he was right of course. My parents would be worried by now, guaranteed. They had probably tried to call me on my cell phone already, which was still switched off.

The only thing was, how come Julian thought of this *now?*

I got up despite my doubts.

"You're right," I said and held on to the back of the chair with both hands. "I'll go do that right now."

Dustin slammed his coffee cup down onto the little saucer.

"So what happened in the forest?"

"Nothing. She got a little scared of the dark," Julian replied in my place.

Maybe it was how he was being patronizing, or his snide tone of voice—or maybe it's just my personality that I constantly have to do things that are totally irrational. No sooner did I want to hold back than I said the words out loud: "I am *not* afraid of the dark. I had very good reasons to be scared."

Maybe I had another good reason now, too, because I had said something that made Julian freeze up while the other two exchanged alarmed glances. Mistake, Eva! In a flash, fear pulled the ground from under me. What if they're really *them*?

Eros Ramazotti had stopped singing on the radio.

Julian jumped to his feet, put an arm around me.

"She saw someone get a little beaten up from far away. He must have screamed, which is what scared her, even though she was very far away, as I said. Then she read that thing about Alina, and that's enough to freak anyone out." He dug his fingers into my ribs. I understood: quit talking.

"Yeah, that Alina thing is pretty bad," said Dustin, "but the fight—what's it to her?"

"Nothing. She got a little spooked, that's all," Julian replied.

"Hmm." Dustin got up.

Mickey got up, too, and as I looked at the two of them in front of me I was back in the woods and could almost feel the beating that boy had received.

"Will you pay for my coffee, Julian? Thanks," Dustin said casually, and I watched helplessly as my boyfriend nodded.

"Thanks for the sugar wafers, dude. Alright, see you tonight. We're counting on you. And look after your girlfriend. She looks like she's gonna keel over."

"Low blood pressure," Julian explained.

If I hadn't been so rattled and exhausted, I would have given them a grin.

They left. We stood there in front of our table and looked down at our half-melted ice cream sundae.

12

"Okay then, so those are my friends...normally they're quite nice. Honestly." Julian smiled a little sheepishly and motioned toward the table. "Don't worry about it. Now let's have some ice cream!"

Or whatever is left of it, I thought, but I didn't say it out loud. Dustin and Mickey had come over us like a thunderstorm.

Because I had somewhat lost my appetite, I decided to disappear into the bathroom for a little while. Standing in the ladies' room in front of the washbowl and splashing my face with cold water, I had some peace and quiet and was able to take a step back, collect my strength, reflect.

It would be quite a coincidence to run into the boys from the forest the next morning. If Julian hadn't acted so strangely just now, I wouldn't have taken my hunch seriously at all. But now, I felt I had no other choice but to talk with him about my suspicions—no matter how much of a gaffe that might turn out to be.

I knew this feeling from my therapy sessions. How often had I tried to keep unpleasant thoughts secret from the fox guy and had, at the same time, known that I would say them out loud sooner or later. And most of the time it wasn't so bad in the end—surely, it must be possible to be straightforward with my *boyfriend* about Dustin and Mickey.

When I returned to the table, Julian had bravely polished off his share of the sundae.

"Feeling better?" he asked.

"Yeah." I sat down next to him. Then I gathered up all my courage and asked the question that I was dying to ask: "Why didn't you want me to talk to them about what happened in the forest?"

"Oh, Evie!" Julian wiped a chocolate sprinkle from his upper lip. "Munkelbach is a village! Everybody knows everybody. Something like this quickly makes the rounds, and I just didn't want the whole world to know."

I raised my eyebrows in disbelief. Was that really the only reason?

Julian shrugged innocently.

"I wanted to protect you. That's why I said go call your parents—which you still haven't done, by the way."

"I'll do it in a minute." Our eyes met. It made me happy that he wanted to protect me.

He noticed this, took my hand, caressed it.

"Don't worry! Just stop talking about it so much, okay?"

"These two friends—" I started, but he interrupted me.

"Please don't worry about them. I mean it! They take a little getting used to, you know. They're a little rough and whatever, but they're totally cool."

"I believe you, I do, but somehow they remind me of those guys in the forest!"

Julian bit his lip. "Dustin and Mickey?" he asked, superfluously. "They wouldn't just beat somebody up like that.

You should know me well enough by now to know that I wouldn't get involved with such a rough crowd."

I didn't reply. I knew Julian as someone who acted with self-confidence, who knew how to defend himself, who held strong personal opinions, and who wouldn't allow anyone to steal a sugar wafer from his ice cream sundae. What I saw now was an insecure little boy who really didn't seem too comfortable in his own skin.

"You don't *want* to think they're capable of something like that, but deep down you kind of think they are," I said boldly and felt like the fox guy when he confronts me with a truth that I don't want to acknowledge.

Julian squirmed, put the spoon aside, and said evasively, "But you're not even sure yourself what you saw last night. It was dark. At least dark enough so they didn't see you. So how can you say that you would recognize them?"

At first I wanted to reply that that wasn't what I had said at all, but then I thought it best not to be too semantic about it so that I wouldn't ruin the mood again.

"Alright, let's not think about it for now," I said instead.

Julian seemed relieved, as if a weight had been lifted off his shoulders.

"Oh yes! Please!" he exclaimed quickly, slipped over to me, and snuggled up to me. "Let's really try to be on vacation from now on, okay?"

"Alright then."

"Kiss it out!"

We sealed our deal. Julian smiled a happy smile, but I still had a stale aftertaste in my mouth. What if I *wasn't* wrong about Dustin and Mickey but wrong about Julian keeping a secret from me?

The mill and the creek were a familiar sight to me now. There was nothing about the place that said "welcome home" to me, but by the time Julian parked his dirt bike I felt reasonably relaxed again. Whether or not Dustin and Mickey were there last night, my boyfriend most certainly did not beat up that unknown boy. He had been sitting here, worriedly waiting for me, and today he even tried to protect me. I was almost delighted when he suggested that we use the groceries we had bought at the market to make a salad. I turned on some happy tunes, called my parents, lied to them with such skill that I myself believed everything was alright, relaxed, swiped some freshly cut mozzarella pieces from under Julian's nose, and managed to be my boisterous, happy-go-lucky self.

After our meal, we had a cappuccino out on the patio. I enjoyed the sunshine, kept watch on a spotted woodpecker that was searching for food up and down the length of a tree, and could have idled out here for a good while longer, but Julian felt the need to go back inside.

It didn't take long for us to end up upstairs. Well, that's why we had come here in the first place, wasn't it? Because we loved each other and wanted to do *it* from the beginning.

All the reasons why I had fallen in love with him were still there, of course: his shy/marveling smile, his bright eyes, full lips, beautiful soft hands, his seductive scent. If there ever was anyone I wanted, it was Julian! While we kissed, everything was wonderful again—as it had been on the day of my departure. I was happy to be in his arms, I felt intense desire for him, I enjoyed how he caressed my face, and yet—

"Everything alright, Evie?"

"Hmm."

"Really?"

"Yeah, of course. You're happy that I'm here, right?"

"Of course!" He let go of me, looked at me dumbfounded. "Why shouldn't I be happy?"

I shrugged, afraid to bring that tiresome topic up again. Obviously, Julian knew what events had caused a crack in our relationship, had hurt our feelings for one another. He nodded, took a deep breath, and said as honestly as he could, "Look, I know that a few things went wrong. But that doesn't change anything about the fact that I'm very happy that you're here. I love you, and I want to be with you!"

"Oh, I know," I exclaimed, and I meant it and didn't mean it at the same time. I snuggled into his arms, allowed him to rock me like a baby at first, and then to slip the straps of my top off my shoulders. How that tickled and tingled! We both had to giggle, and I savored the moment. And suddenly I really wanted *it* to happen, right here, right now. I wanted to be very close to Julian, against my doubts, against my anger, against my fear.

"How can you even think that I'm not happy about you being here. I'm the luckiest guy on earth," Julian whispered, his nose pressed into the little hollow between my collarbones, his lips on my skin, his voice barely comprehensible, only audible to my heart.

I didn't reply, gazed at his closed eyes, allowed the deep relaxation that was showing on his face to spread all over me, and ran my fingers through his short, unruly hair. I thought back to all the hours we'd spent cuddling with mounting passion in his or my room, in the park, in the movie theater—always worried that someone might come in or walk by, disrupting us. We had been looking forward to this weekend, had yearned for this very moment. I didn't want anything to spoil it, wanted to blank out what had happened, wanted to erase my mental hard drive.

Julian pulled my top over my head. For just a moment, I was startled as he started kissing my breasts. So the moment had finally arrived; we would do *it*, now, and it scared me a little. Julian noticed what was going on, hesitated, gave me an inquisitive look. Maybe he was unsure himself, was having similar thoughts.

"I love you," I said softly, for him, for me, for us both. And when I saw the relieved look in his eyes, I knew that it was true. Of course, I had seen aspects of his character in the past few hours that I found irritating and that proved to me that he wasn't anywhere near as perfect as I thought he would be. But the fact that Julian, my hero, had certain weaknesses, too, made me almost like him more. I wrapped my arms around him and started, in my turn, undressing him. His hands and kisses banished any final worries. Besides, there was only enough room for our warm bodies underneath that blanket.

For a long time afterward, we just lay there, together, bodies entwined, while the blanket had long since slipped to the floor. I was happy, though not as overwhelmingly happy as I thought I would be. Much more important than that was the fact that I had done *it*, and that *it* had been good, had been nice. I felt as if I had taken another step toward my liberation and independence. I had been afraid of my first time, and now I was proud that I had tried and discovered it for myself. As silly as it may sound, right now I felt like I had when I'd learned how to read and suddenly the entire world of books had opened up. I cuddled up to Julian, listened to his slowing breaths, pulled the blanket back up and over us, and—feeling a strange mix of budding optimism, of yearning for distant places, and of delicious sleepiness—gazed out at the mountains of clouds drifting by our window.

13

This very special event was in fact worthy of an entry in my journal. I could of course write it down—I had a new diary now—but what if I were able to find the old one?

Julian was sound asleep. It wouldn't take long. I would just return to the spot where I had gotten lost; ten minutes, twenty minutes max, and I'd be back. Maybe he wouldn't even notice. I slipped my hand out of his and very quietly got up from the bed. I still had this strange feeling in my belly: alien, grown-up. I glanced at my body in the wardrobe mirror. Even though I looked a little disheveled, what with my flushed cheeks and tousled hair, I thought I was prettier than ever. I was a fantastic woman, so there!

And Julian, sweet Julian, was still the best boy in the whole entire world! He was snoring a little, turned over on his belly and hugging his pillow. Since he had something to cuddle up to, maybe he wouldn't miss me too much.

I got dressed quickly, snuck down the stairs and out the patio door. Vollmer's cat came and rubbed up against my legs. I briefly petted her black, sun-warmed fur, which she thanked me for with a luxurious purr, and then I set out, wearing a hoodie and sneakers, as if I wanted to go for a run after my lover and I had just... Boy, was I proud of myself!

Walking through the forest made me take special notice of how full of energy and how happy I was. I took off like a skyrocket, sang, jumped over tree roots—and shrieked when I suddenly found myself face-to-face with a police officer and his German shepherd dog.

"Don't be scared!" the gray-haired man said, giving a little smile and commanding his dog to sit down beside him. "Where're you off to? Munkelbach?"

"Yes, uh, no, I mean, I lost something here yesterday. A diary."

"A diary?" he asked, astounded. It was only then that I noticed that he wasn't out here on his own; I saw several more officers combing the forest a little distance away. "We're searching for a missing girl." His voice sounded extremely serious, as if I should be ashamed for wasting time on something so trivial as a diary.

"Oh God, of course!" I had forgotten all about Alina, that missing girl! And right away the forest seemed like a threat to me—and my decision to set out on my own seemed very reckless and stupid. "I read about it in the newspaper."

"Are you from Munkelbach? You know this girl?" The police officer produced a notebook as a matter of routine and motioned to his colleagues that he was questioning me and would catch up to them later.

"No, I only got here last night. I'm on vacation with my boyfriend, in the Rauschenmühle water mill."

"Vollmer?"

"What? No! With Julian Wende! His parents are renting an apartment there."

The police officer nodded and asked for my name and age. I replied mechanically, all the while wondering how this man could possibly assume that Vollmer, the weird landlord, was my *boyfriend*.

"You lost your diary here in the forest?"

"Yes, on my way from the railroad station to the mill. I was in a real hurry; my backpack must have ripped open, and my journal fell out."

"Hmm. Didn't your boyfriend pick you up?"

"He sprained his ankle."

It all sounded strangely implausible, even though it was true.

"Ah. Did you notice anything special?"

"Uh, well…" I hesitated for a moment, and the police officer—he seemed to have the same instinct as the fox guy did—noticed immediately.

"Every little detail might be helpful, no matter how small. Don't forget, we're looking for a girl your age," he reminded me. "She could be a friend of yours."

"Yeah, but this definitely had nothing to do with it," I said hurriedly. "There was a fight, or rather, there were these four youths beating up this one guy. I really wanted to help him, but…" In two, three sentences, I described the scene at the rain shelter. I didn't forget to tell them that Julian and I had gone back later to help the boy if necessary, and I also mentioned how unsure I was about the seriousness of the incident. "My boyfriend says it probably wasn't all that bad. We had a big fight about it."

"Hmm," the police officer said again. "Here in Munkelbach, we haven't really had any acts of physical violence among youths, but I'm fully aware that we no longer live in a fairytale world, not even out here in the country. I will let my fellow officers know. If you remember anything else about this, please get in touch. Even if the case of the missing girl is more pressing right now, we mustn't ignore something like that." He gave me a friendly nod. "And if I may give you a piece of advice…I don't mean to scare you, but please ask your boyfriend to help you look for your diary."

"I understand." I had no business being out here in the forest. Julian was probably waiting already. "Good-bye," I said, unsure if such a trivial phrase was even appropriate. Most of all, though, I was glad that I could now turn around and run back to the mill.

14

"Where have you been?" Julian was already out on the courtyard patio and walked toward me. He seemed agitated. "I wake up and you're gone!"

"Sorry. Did you sleep well?" I asked extra nicely. "I just wanted to go look for my journal real quick."

"Oh, you and your stupid diary! You've got a new one now!"

"But still," I countered. "My notes have great sentimental value to me! People keep their old pictures, don't they, even if they buy a new camera?" I could feel just how much I was enjoying this. "By the way, the police are searching the forest for that girl your friends were talking about. They're combing the entire area. They asked me if I'd seen anything, and I told them about that fight in the woods."

I should have known that Julian wouldn't be particularly thrilled about such news.

"Why would you do that?" he called out and threw his hands up over his head. "Holy cow! She goes to the cops! It's none of their business!" He made the cuckoo sign with his index finger and seemed to make a big deal out of it. "Didn't I tell you not to go around telling everyone?!"

He scared me half to death, but at the same time, I was getting angry. My own fears and mistakes aside, but you really had to start wondering what exactly was wrong with Julian! I didn't know him to explode in such anger. In the six weeks we'd been together, he had never been so irritable and quick-tempered, not once. So were these his true colors now, the ones that he would only show after spending more than two or three hours together?

"Look, I can just go home to my parents," I said as coolly as I could muster. That's what I should have done. Pack my things and go, right there and then.

"Yeah, whatever. Why don't you just go home!" Julian screamed. If I hadn't seen tears shimmering in his eyes, I really would have left. I was *this* close, hesitated for only a split second.

Right at that point, Bernd Vollmer walked onto the patio. He seemed to be in a bad mood.

"Jesus Christ, enough with all the yelling already! Can't you take your little lovers' quarrel inside?! It's unbearable! And Julian, how many times do I have to tell you not to park your dirt bike right in the middle of the garage so that I'm always having to maneuver like ten times!"

"Yes, Mr. Vollmer, I'll remember next time." My boyfriend wiped his eyes and stuck out his chin.

The man turned toward me. "You don't like it here, huh?"

Did I hear mockery in his voice? Vollmer put his hands on his hips and looked me over. Even though Julian had described him as a total creep to me, I had to admit that he wasn't exactly unattractive in broad daylight: athletic, tanned, with honey-colored hair that was a little *too* tousled for someone who was such a neat freak. He was younger than I had imagined and wearing casual, relaxed clothes—washed-out denim jeans with bright paint splashed all over them, and a plaid flannel shirt with the sleeves rolled up to his elbows so that I noticed the big, bloody scratch on his forearm right away.

Vollmer followed my gaze. "Trimming the hedges, fixing the roof, planting rosebushes. *Somebody* has to take care of the mill. The boys here sure don't lift a finger! Instead, they steal roses and marigolds right from under my kitchen window, and whenever I ask Mr. Wende here to feed my cat for three days because we're out of town, he can't even handle that."

"Midnight was doing just fine. There're enough mice around here." Julian folded his arms across his chest and disappeared into the house.

I didn't budge. Vollmer had fixed the roof? By himself? I mean, without Julian's help? Was I getting this right?

"You haven't said a single word, young lady!" He pulled down his sleeves, giving me a grin. There was something provocative in his eyes.

"Are you afraid to speak your own mind?"

I would have liked to come back with something cool and witty, but I couldn't make a sound. Vollmer looked at me with such furious anger that I got goose bumps. Why? What was his problem with me? Was he really secretly a sadist, as Julian had said? He didn't seem to expect a reply from me but instead turned around and headed back to his apartment.

Above him, in a window on the second floor, I saw a shadowy silhouette behind the curtains. The young male disappeared as soon as he noticed my gaze.

Who was that? Wasn't that the boy from the forest? Was he Vollmer's son? Wow, then it would make sense why his dad had scowled at me! And it also would make sense why he had taken his hunting rifle with him last night. He probably didn't want to go hunting at all—but to find and protect his son!

I stormed into the house. Julian had taken a seat on the couch and folded his arms across his chest. He seemed exhausted. I think he intended his first words to sound like he was trying to make peace. "Did you at least find your diary?"

"No." Determined to find answers to all these many questions inside my head, I sat down in the armchair opposite him. "Julian, does Vollmer by any chance have a son?"

"How the heck do you know that?"

"I saw him in the window."

"So? What about him? He doesn't matter. He's ten times the idiot his father is. People here in town at least have respect for Bernd because he's the assistant principal at the high school. Mirko is a nobody, a total loser. No one pays any attention to him. That's why I didn't mention him to you."

"But it would have been nice. Because I got scared when I suddenly saw him standing there."

"Seems to me you get scared pretty much all the time," Julian countered.

This knocked the wind right out of my sails. You bet I did—getting scared and freaking out was my specialty, so to speak. I was silent and knotted my fingers together as I always do during my sessions with the fox guy.

Julian looked very nervous himself. The atmosphere was so tense that I feared I'd get a headache shortly.

Finally, I couldn't take our silence any longer and said what I needed to say: "Julian, I think Mirko is the boy your friends were beating up last night. And I also think that his dad overheard our conversation last night and went to get Mirko from the forest."

"Oh boy!" Julian was pulling his hair, looking almost desperate now.

For a moment, I was afraid he would present a thousand irrefutable arguments against my suspicions, only to declare how full-on crazy I was. I probably would have been more than happy to believe anything he said, even though by now I was sure that I had pieced everything together correctly.

Because if I was right and if Julian's friends really had beaten up the landlord's son, then this would be extremely awkward for Julian, too. Even if it turned out that he had nothing to do with the dispute, Bernd Vollmer would almost certainly not like him any better. The question was, though, whether he really had nothing to do with the quarrel. Julian hadn't beaten Mirko up, I was sure of that. At the time in question he was nursing his very dubious foot injury on the brightly lit patio, an injury he had sustained while fixing the roof—but Bernd insisted that he himself, not Julian, had fixed the roof. Was it possible that Julian had invented the foot-injury story just to have an alibi to present to Bernd? If Bernd knew that Julian was sitting at home with an injury while the gang was attacking his son, he would have nothing to pin on him and wouldn't be able to, say, terminate his parents' lease. But by extension, this also meant that Julian hadn't picked me up from the railroad station simply because he knew that his four friends were planning an attack on Mirko.

This was an outrageous thought.

Julian opened his mouth. He would disagree, provide an explanation. And I would sit here looking like an idiot, an overanxious teenager with way too much imagination who didn't trust her own boyfriend because she was almost incapable of interacting with other people and had only learned how to do this in therapy.

He said, "Please, Evie, understand. My friends here are important to me, and it doesn't matter what you think of them—they are good guys."

I gasped for breath like a swimmer who has been swimming under water for a long time and was coming up for air. That was a pretty weak explanation, wasn't it?

"Yesterday, in the forest, I saw what your friends are like," I started timidly.

Julian shook his head violently. "But it was dark, wasn't it?"

Suddenly, I saw the fox guy sitting before me, and how he would slap his hand down on his knee in outrage. "Stop putting up with everything! Defend yourself! Break something sometime, express your anger!" This memory gave me a burst of energy.

"Stop talking to me like I'm an idiot!" I suddenly yelled at Julian, feeling tears shoot into my eyes with full force. At the same time, I felt as strong as ever. "I get the feeling you know more than you're telling me, and I think that's very wrong! Especially after everything that happened earlier today. You know what? I feel like I'm being taken for a ride. I think I'll really just go home to my parents."

Julian hadn't expected such an outburst from me. He looked on in horror, didn't make a sound. I took a determined look at my wristwatch. Twenty to five. Enough daylight left to pack my bags and walk through the forest back to the railroad station. Or maybe I would call a taxicab this time; I had plenty of vacation money left.

"No," Julian begged me just then. "Wait! Don't go! You're right. I really didn't tell you everything. Mirko and my friends don't get along. It's always been like that, and as someone who lives under the same roof as Mirko, I'm constantly caught in the middle, even if I don't do anything. If yesterday my friends smacked him around a little, then that doesn't mean that they're violent or whatever, or that they were doing it without a good reason. You have to believe me, please! Yeah, okay, so maybe I was being a little bit of a jerk, but only because I didn't want to get into trouble! I was so looking forward to our weekend together, planned everything down to the last detail. I simply made a mistake, and—"

"What kind of a mistake?" I wanted to know but didn't receive an answer straightaway. Instead, Julian himself was fighting back tears, slipped from his armchair, crawled over to me, clung to my knees.

"A mistake, many mistakes! To invite you here of all places. To not pick you up. To not tell you about Mirko and my circle of friends. I was such a coward! But you—you're the most genuine and honest person that I know. My friends here, they're easygoing and all, and you can have lots of fun with them, go totally crazy, but with you—with you I know that the feelings are real. I can feel that you're scared and that sometimes you don't feel well. That's why I didn't want you to get all stressed out. All I wanted was for you to have a great time here; I wanted to keep you away from all of this. Because I love you, Eva! Oh, everything would have been amazing if only your train had been on time."

I was quite happy to believe him, but things had happened, hadn't they? His plan had gone wrong, and I had gotten myself into a story that I was unable to guess the end of. At any rate, this was a story I didn't like at all. My mind told me loud and clear to go pack my bags. On the other hand, I so longed for a happy ending; I felt that I deserved it after being on my own for so long. After all, Julian was my first love.

"Please stay! When I woke up earlier and you weren't here, I was crazy worried. I thought I'd hurt you or did something wrong. I...you know, it was my first time, too."

I ran my hand through his hair. Julian let out a blissful sigh and looked me straight in the eye.

"But you did enjoy it, despite everything? You don't regret it, do you?"

I nodded and shook my head all at the same time, allowed him to whisper sweet compliments into my ear, nuzzle me, woo me. If he continued on like that, my plan to bring light into this whole big mess would go right out the window. What about the roof, then, or his foot? Was everything really exactly as I imagined it to be? Did I really need to be 100 percent sure? Couldn't I just accept Julian's apology?

I was so torn. I knew that I couldn't allow myself to be drawn in by his pretty words. But at the same time, I was worried about getting too caught up in my suspicions.

If only I could ask someone—my parents, or Sarah. But a phone call would—if I even managed to get hold of someone—take forever, and in the end I really ought to find the answer by myself.

"Give me another chance, Evie! I was being unfair, but I promise I won't do it again. Please, please don't go home!"

I smiled a little. "Can you read my mind?"

"Sometimes." He pressed me against him. "And sometimes I'm so dumb that I don't even get what's going on inside my own head."

I liked that. Didn't the saying go, "Innocent until proven guilty?" I made a decision. "Okay, fine, I'll stay."

"Thank you. I'm glad. You know, that's what I like about you: that you don't just throw in the towel when things get a little tough, that you're not giving up."

I blushed a little. The truth was this: even if I wanted to give up, I couldn't. When I had called my parents earlier today at lunchtime, they had said how happy they were for me to be striking out on my own and managing so well. I really didn't want to disappoint them or the fox guy, who had said that I was on the right track. I also stayed put because I really, desperately, needed to prove something to myself.

"Can you promise me just one thing?" Julian asked. "Could you please not go into the forest by yourself anymore?"

I gave a little start, thought about the missing girl and the police officer. "Alright," I replied.

"I really barely know Alina," Julian said quietly, leaning his back against my legs and staring at the colorful children's drawings covering the wall. "You see the pictures there? I know that Alina paints. She showed me her portfolio once.

I totally liked it. Super powerful, bright colors, like you're looking at a kaleidoscope. You know what I mean?"

I nodded, but Julian didn't even take notice. "Laura, of course, claims that Alina paints these things only when she's stoned, but it's not true. Laura's just jealous. Alina makes paintings that drive away the cobwebs, you know? You should always carry one of her paintings with you as your emergency kit, or you could maybe buy them in a drugstore as medication for sadness and bad moods."

"Interesting idea. Maybe someone should suggest that to her."

"Yeah," Julian laughed, looking miserable. "Let's just hope the police won't find anything bad."

We remained silent and found it difficult to start over with our conversation. Why? Were we having doubts that Alina would continue with her art and sell her paintings? A strange mood suddenly filled the air; the sun was shining into the living room but no longer carried any warmth, and a moment later, it was swallowed up by a cloud.

15

"Oh please, come with me! I can't cancel on them, and I'm not going to stay long, either." Julian bent down and threw a handful of small pebbles into the water that was glistening in the evening light. We were sitting on a bench by the riverside, behind us the mill, before us the bridge we expected his friends to appear on any moment now. The rest of the afternoon had been so nice: quiet, harmonious, with lots of cuddling—exactly as this vacation was supposed to be. That's why I somehow hoped that Julian would cancel the evening with his group of friends. But I was wrong.

"You wanted to see the area. So, we'll just drive around with them for an hour or so and have a barbecue by the castle ruins. It's very romantic there and"—Julian play-acted as if to scare me— "spooky!" He breathed "woo, woo" several times into my ear and then started to tenderly suck on it.

"Really?" My need for excitement and spookiness was more than satisfied at this stage. I also felt a little uneasy already. Our picnic basket contained a lot more things to drink than things to eat, and the thought of having to spend an entire evening with cocky Mickey and grumpy Dustin did not seem very appealing to me. Plus, my memories of the previous evening made it even worse. The off-road vehicle coming over the bridge was exactly the same one I had seen the night before, and the jacket of the third boy, who got out of the car with Mickey and Dustin and shook Julian's hand amicably, read: *Munkelbach 79 Sports & Athletics Club–Team Handball.* Now I regretted not having gone home. I felt stupid. Inexcusably weak, naïve, and gullible.

For a while, I just stood there by the bench. My mouth was dry, my heart was racing. My hair stood on end. I couldn't walk up to these people, I couldn't. I didn't want anything to do with the likes of them. Those were not "friends." I pressed my palms together in strained concentration. I didn't want to go with them, but what could I do? Let Julian go by himself and lock myself in the mill? Take my freshly recharged cell phone and call my parents? And then what? They wouldn't be able to get here on such short notice. It was too far from there to Munkelbach.

"Eva, come here and bring the basket!"

Stiffly, I walked over to the car. The third boy introduced himself as Chris. I shook his hand and said my name.

"Are the girls coming directly to the ruins?" Julian asked.

"Yeah. Laura passed her test this morning. Thankfully, I'm no longer the only one here with a car who has to drive everyone else around." Chris held the door for me, and I sat down in the back beside Mickey. Julian followed suit.

"Laura must have bribed the examiner. I can't imagine how else she would pass her driver's test," Mickey called against the loud music. He smelled a little of beer already, and I really didn't like having to sit next to him.

Julian seemed to have noticed; at least he clasped his hand around mine. "Technically, Laura should be buying a round, too," he said.

"And so should you, Julian," grumbled Dustin. "It's your turn eventually, isn't it?"

"Come on, I already paid for the football tickets!"

Silently, I followed the guys' conversation, staring at Julian's hand—my life support—for the entire time. He was my boyfriend, but I knew nothing of his life here. He hadn't even told me that he was interested in football, and I had no idea what to expect this evening.

"That was just the advance payment on our little plan," Dustin muttered with an unlit cigarette in his mouth. "But the situation has changed since this morning. So, I mean, you need to throw in some more cash."

Julian's hand clenched tighter around mine. "Sure, we can talk about this, but just don't worry about it too much. Nothing happened."

"Dude, something keeps happening all day long," Mickey exclaimed, slapping his hands, as if it was a joke, on his and my thighs—right hand on his, left hand on mine—and laughed like an idiot. He was either pretty drunk already, or maybe he acted like a clown all the time.

"Oh hey, does anyone have any news on Alina?" Chris asked.

"My mom was at Irene's earlier, and she won't stop crying and stuff," Dustin reported. "You know, she doesn't believe that her daughter has run away. She did it twice before, but these past few weeks she's been getting along just fine with her parents."

Chris agreed.

"Before, Alina would always say that she wanted to leave and get as far away from Munkelbach as possible. But not lately. Only two weeks ago my sister said that, after high school, she'd probably have to go traveling by herself."

"Huh, certainly looks like it," Dustin growled darkly.

"I think they've started looking for Alina *everywhere*," Mickey declared.

"That's right, the police were here in the woods earlier," Julian said. "Eva saw them."

"Really? So?"

Suddenly, I felt all eyes on me. I raised my head. I was squeezed in between three thugs and my dishonest boyfriend. Much of it reminded me of the situation last night. The off-road vehicle had gone off the main road and was tearing along a forest road. It was already dark below the trees, and even the music was the same.

I gathered spit in my mouth, strained to answer as quickly and naturally as possible. "Nothing! I was looking for something."

"Did you tell the cops about that fight that you saw? Come on, be honest," Mickey said and moved in even closer. "You told them, didn't you?"

"How could she have known it was you!" Julian almost yelled. "She's always trying to help. She wanted to call the police and the paramedics last night, but I didn't tell her that we were friends. I tried to keep her out of it. She figured it all out anyway, but she won't tell anyone, she's my girlfriend; you can take my word for it. Jeez, you should be glad that it was Eva who saw you and not someone else!"

His words felt like a punch to my stomach. While I had suspected this, being told right to my face was an altogether different story. So Julian had known all along! It was crystal-clear, then, why he had so vehemently refused to help the injured boy, and what the story was with his alleged sprained ankle. I could even picture who he had called from the garage.

I was just sitting there, paralyzed; everything went black. Vertigo wanted to come, but I wouldn't allow it, not now; I had to keep my head clear, I needed to hold on to something, even if it was Julian's hand.

"Who says we can trust her?" Dustin asked skeptically. Oh God, how could my boyfriend do this to me—me, the only witness—and throw me to the wolves?!

"Me! I'm telling you!" Julian squeezed my hand almost to a pulp. "Eva is alright."

Chris stopped the car on a forest parking lot and turned off the music. The sudden silence was oppressive. I sat there, frozen in shock.

"Okay, Julian, you'll take care of this, okay?" Dustin said. He seemed to be the one calling the shots in this group of friends. "You know what you've got to lose! Alright then, I'm counting on you." He got out, stood beside the car, and lit a cigarette.

"Wow, this went all kinds of wrong, dude!" Mickey said and got out, too, as a second car pulled into the parking lot.

Julian and I stayed in our seats, silently. My heart was still beating. A scary thought: as long as I was alive, someone could hurt me.

Chris turned around to face us.

"The two of them are pretty cranky. They're worried that Vollmer could stop them from graduating. I'm not taking any classes with him, so nothing can happen to me in that sense. But still, I'd feel better, too, if he didn't have it in for us. It would be best for everyone if you stayed out of this, Eva."

"Yes," I murmured.

"She is," Julian said.

"Alright. Ah, there's Emra, Laura, and Olga." Chris gave a crooked smile. "Now stop peeing your pants, already. We're friends; we will sort this out. Nothing is ever as bad as it looks."

Chris left the car and, once outside, said hello to the girls. Julian made no move to get up; he was as still as I was and kept holding on to my hand. Finally—two of the girls had knocked on the car windows in the meantime—he said with a great deal of remorse, "I'm so sorry, Eva. This is not what I wanted. You know, my friends are pretty alright, and this guy, this Mirko, he really deserves it. I mean…"

"Hey, what's up with the two of you? Are you afraid of the dark?" One of the girls—this must be Laura, judging by her hair color—flung open the car door. She was wearing a lot of makeup, and she came across as someone who was used to being constantly admired and worshipped. "Julian!" she called, pulling him away from me, from the car, and hugging him excessively. "Hi! How's your foot?" She roared with laughter.

Julian grinned sheepishly and threw me an apologetic glance. "This is Eva," he introduced me, and I had no choice but to get out of the car. I felt like a snail that was being pulled from her protective shell by an albino crab with nail-polish-red pincers.

"I thought as much. So, Eva, I didn't see you last night. Where were you hiding? Behind the porta-potty?" Giggling, she covered her mouth with her hand, and if I hadn't been so paralyzed and all alone in the world I would have loved to give her a good ol' smack right across her slutty face.

But I had my own issues to deal with. Feverishly, I tried to remember what the fox guy had advised me for situations such as this. I couldn't think of a single thing; my mind was completely blank. He had of course assumed that I would never encounter any real danger. But I had now, hadn't I? I overheard Dustin telling Mickey that anyone who would try to tell on him would live to regret it. Okay, he was referring to cheating on his exam papers, but because he was looking over to me—directly, menacingly—I had to assume that he was also giving me a hint with a baseball bat. Hopefully, Dustin didn't realize that Mirko's dad probably already knew what had happened. I thought he was perfectly capable of taking his anger out on me, whether or not I was "staying out of it." The only thing—despite this enormous strain— that helped me stay beside Julian rather than run away, upright and seemingly unimpressed on the outside, was the thought that one day, within the next hour, sometime soon, I'd be able to tell the fox guy all about it.

The group got moving, and Julian and I with it. We took a hiking trail that wound its way up a densely wooded hill. At times, we felt the warm, reddish evening sun on our faces; at other times, we could feel the shadowy chill of this October evening. Laura, who was ill equipped for a forest hike in her high heels, was complaining nonstop. There were two other girls with us apart from her: a pretty Turkish girl who was having a lively discussion with Chris; and skinny, brown-haired Olga, who seemed to be Dustin's girlfriend and was right for him insofar as she wasn't talking much.

The little workout did me good. I had to pay attention to where I put my feet and therefore had to quit my nonstop thinking about what had happened and what else might happen.

After fifteen minutes, we reached the top. The castle ruins, parts of which had been restored and reinforced, were gleaming in the light of the setting sun. Technically, a beautiful spot.

"Great view, huh?" Chris came over to me, nudged me, and said, "Oh, come on, smile a little!" He then asked me to climb up on a wall with him. "Down there, that's Munkelbach. That ugly complex of buildings in front, on the slope, that's our school complex. It's a little out of town, only a few minutes from here. In clear weather, you can see all the way up to the Mosel River, but it's too hazy now. The forecast says that it'll be quite cloudy tomorrow."

"Hey Chris, are you playing tour guide?" Laura teased him, but he was unfazed and explained that Ravenwood Castle was *the* romantic place to be during the summer.

"This is where I got my first kiss," confirmed Emra, who was setting the picnic area and had started unpacking drinks, chips, and cookies together with Olga.

"Really? Who was it?" asked Laura.

"Not important."

"Come on, you have to tell us now!"

"Exactly, Emra. We're curious. You know how we're always interested in your little indiscretions!" Mickey wanted to put his arm around her shoulders, but she pushed him away.

"Why don't you go and light the fire. We also have music, right?"

"Don't change the subject, Emra," Laura demanded. "Who was it? And I'll tell you who my first was!"

"No, it's a secret."

"Probably Mirko!" Mickey exclaimed tauntingly, prompting Emra to shriek, jump to her feet, and chase him across the entire picnic area.

"Mirko is Vollmer's son, you know, the guy you saw yesterday," Chris explained.

"Nobody likes him," Julian added. This was the first thing he'd said in a long time. "Emra would definitely not have kissed *him*. No girl would voluntarily kiss him."

I said nothing.

"You know, he's not only a know-it-all, but he's also not a very nice guy." It seemed as if Julian now wanted to play catch-up with all these extra explanations. "He snoops around, spies on his classmates to get teachers to like him."

And how would *you* know, I thought. You don't live here, you only hear what other people tell you, and you repeat it like a parrot.

"He was dumb even when he was little. In the beginning, when we rented our holiday home for the first time, he would always run after me. He got on my nerves, always sticking to me like glue."

"He's gay, dude!" Mickey exclaimed with satisfaction, as if he had just pulled off some kind of brilliant intellectual achievement. He then ripped open a can of beer and handed it over to an angry Emra, saying, "Calm down already! I take it back! Come on, let me light the fire!"

"He's got issues *upstairs*, Eva, believe me." Julian rolled his eyes and waved his hands in front of his face. "Like I said, he really deserves it, he—"

"Why?" I yelled at him. "Because he's different?" I sure didn't want to turn my boyfriend against me in addition to everyone else, but I was more than a little familiar with people who are wired differently.

"Because he's deliberately trying to hurt and harm others," Olga said quietly, yet in a sharp, biting tone that was clear enough for everyone to hear. Maybe it was because this was the first thing this girl had said all day; at any rate, nobody tried to crack any silly jokes in response.

"That's right." Emra handed the can back to Mickey without having drunk any beer herself, and she motioned for us to get down from the wall. "Sit down and help yourselves. And then I will tell Eva why I'm very grateful that you guys taught Mirko Vollmer a lesson last night."

16

Mickey and Dustin lit twigs and pieces of paper, and we sat down on blankets that Olga and Emra had spread out on the lawn. The sun had almost set by now, the sky was gray, and there was a halo around the moon that seemed to confirm the change in weather Chris had predicted. Even if it might snow tomorrow, what did I care? This had stopped being a vacation a long time ago.

Everyone smoked except for me. Even Julian allowed Laura to light one for him—and I didn't even know that he cared for cigarettes. Everyone was drinking alcohol, too; only Emra seemed to be just nipping from the wine, and I was glad that, although I was offered some, nobody was trying to make me drink.

"So, Eva, listen: It was Mirko who started all of this, not us. He took a picture of me while I was making out with a boy at the school party."

"So who was it?" Mickey asked in the same tone of voice Laura had used to show her curiosity earlier. But this time, nobody seemed to think it was funny; on the contrary, Laura barked at him, "Shut up already!"

"We both had a lot to drink; it didn't mean anything. We were just in the *mood*."

"Hopefully you're in the mood more often, Emra."

"Mickey!" Julian now barked at him in his turn. "Can't you just leave her alone for one second?!"

"Careful, dude," Mickey countered. "Yesterday I *acted* while you were waiting around for your little gem, what with your foot up on a stool and all."

I bit my lip. How come everyone else was in the know except for me?

"It was a German boy, not a Turkish boy. That's all I'm going to say. That's all my dad would be interested in, anyway. You should know that my parents are very liberal, they are, but if they see these photos…"

Emra stopped. Olga put an arm around her, and even Laura, who I didn't think capable of such a compassionate gesture, moved closer to her friend to help console her.

"He was blackmailing her," Olga explained. "Yesterday, in computer science class, he suddenly had this smirk on his face, and then he uploaded three photos to the school server and printed them. He was having a ball; he threatened to send the pictures to Emra's family. If my parents saw such pictures of *me*, all hell would break loose, but I can't even begin to imagine what it would be like for her family. For Muslims, this is an insult to their honor or something."

I nodded, I had heard of this before. I understood why Emra was so worried. She seemed very nice and likeable to me; I was sure she was telling the truth. But still. Somehow, I still had the feeling that this closely-knit group of friends was hiding something from me.

"We were able to make him delete the file in school," Emra explained and wiped a tear from her face. "But he wouldn't hand over his camera phone, and it was during class, so we couldn't make a big fuss about it. He's probably copied the photos to his own computer by now."

"Unfortunately, we only noticed that he had taken pictures with his cell phone when it was too late," Julian said. "He did it on the sly. So typical of Mirko; he's such a rat. He's one of those people you don't even notice, you do it subconsciously, you know. You're thinking: Today is such a beautiful day, I'm going to ignore all these horrible people."

That's why Mirko had mentioned a cell phone! For a moment, I was tempted to bring up it, but I managed to stop myself just in time. Even if I wasn't under attack right now, it was better not to willfully draw attention to myself. It was bad enough that I had been witness to an act of revenge.

"It's so unfair!" Emra exclaimed, close to tears. "You know, if I had ever done anything to him, if I bullied him or picked on him like everyone else at our school, I could maybe understand! But I've never done *anything* to him! He has absolutely no reason whatsoever to mess with me!"

"He won't mess with you. We will mess with him. And he knows." Dustin took a drink from his beer and crossed his arms across his chest.

"Do you see, Evie, why we couldn't call the police yesterday, and why I had to play it all down?" Julian asked me.

"Now you know the whole backstory." Chris gave me an encouraging nod. "I hope you think better of us now."

I was relieved that he sided with me. Even though Julian seemed to do this in his own way, too, I had the feeling that I could rely on and trust Chris even more.

"Laura, go show Eva the photos that Mirko slipped Emra, so that she knows what we're talking about!"

"Oh, come on, just leave it, Mickey. That's so unnecessary. I think she's getting the idea! My girlfriend's not stupid." Julian put his arm around me. "She's all for justice,
and now she knows whose side justice is on. Right, baby?"
He kissed me on the mouth.

I allowed it, happy that I didn't need to take a stand.
With one hand I held on to his and with the other I took the
three badly printed photos that Laura now handed over to
me anyway. Even though the prints were in A4 letter-size for-
mat, I had to strain—thanks to Julian's tighter and tighter
embrace—to recognize anything in them. Besides, it was
getting dark in the picnic area, and while our little blazing
fire gave off enough light, it was breaking my concentration
with its flickering glow.

What I could make out, though partially hidden by
party guests standing in front of her, was Emra with her
eyes closed, red lipstick mouth, sexy open lips, and teasing-
ly stuck-out tongue. It was a silly picture in and of itself,
a harmless attempt at posing like a *Playboy* cover girl that
my parents would have dismissed as a joke—if there hadn't
been a boy sitting behind her on a table, with his legs
wrapped around her belly from behind, his hands on her
breasts. Only the boy's hands, his brown hair, one sneaker,
and parts of his jeans were visible. His head was resting
on Emra's shoulders, and he almost entirely disappeared
behind her back. In the second picture, his hands had
pushed up Emra's top a little; in the third picture, she
had turned around to face him, and an observer could ven-
ture a guess that more than just a small piece of top might
well have been involved.

I was burning up from the inside. Who was that boy? Was it Julian? Was this his brown hair? Were those his sneakers? Julian wore such sneakers, that much I knew. But that didn't mean anything. Thousands of teenage boys wore brand-name sneakers of exactly that type—Dustin and Chris, for example; and Chris, at the very least, also had brown hair. Had Julian been in Munkelbach that evening? And if so, would he, as an outsider, have attended a student-only school party? Surely not…

"When was this picture taken?" I asked cautiously. If Emra replied with "last Saturday," then everything would be alright. Julian and I had gone to the movies last Saturday.

"Tuesday, at the school party. That's also the evening Alina was seen last," Chris replied.

"I can't remember if she was even there that night," Emra said.

"Yeah, she was there, alright." That was Dustin.

"If only you could predict something like this happening, you know, that someone might go missing," Laura suddenly spluttered. "I ran into her in the bathroom, she bummed a cigarette off me, and then she left. And me being such a gossip, I said to Cindy how shitty Alina looked in her denim skirt, super fat legs. 'Miniskirt meets maxi legs,' is what I said, and at that exact moment she came back in because she had left her purse on the windowsill, and she overheard me!"

"Oh, Laura!" Chris put his face in his hands. Dustin grimaced disapprovingly; only Mickey laughed out loud. It was impossible to miss that he was, by now, quite drunk. "You've put your foot in your mouth once again!"

"Yeah. Normally I wouldn't care, I really don't give a damn, but this really *is* weird—now that I know what happened to her and stuff!"

I switched off at that point. I wasn't interested in any of this. All I cared about was whether my boyfriend had been making out with Emra. What little was visible of the boy in the photo was not enough to really recognize who it was. If I could detect Julian in the background, if I could spot him somewhere in the crowd, talking with Mickey and Dustin, I'd feel reassured. It was bad enough that he had been telling me a pack of lies about that fight. I huddled closer to the fire and kept staring at the photos. Please, I thought, please make it so that Julian told me the truth—at least the truth about this one point!

Meanwhile, the conversation about the missing girl, Alina, was getting more and more heated. Emra, Olga, Chris, and Dustin seemed so seriously worried about Alina that even Laura caught on to it in her own brash, superficial way, which in turn prompted Mickey to make wisecracks so as to downplay the situation. Even Julian had his share to say, which was good because it meant that I had a few minutes to myself to concentrate on the photos. No, I couldn't see Julian anywhere, no matter how hard I tried. I searched and I wished, all to no avail. The only familiar face I was able to make out was that of the Rauschenmühle mill's landlord, of all people: Vollmer. Wasn't he a teacher at the school, wasn't that what they had said? Of course. This must be the reason why Mirko was so unpopular: a teacher's kid always has a hard time.

Vollmer was talking to a not-quite-skinny girl in a miniskirt whose face I only saw in profile, but she, too, seemed familiar to me. Miniskirt and maxi legs: Alina?

I leaned even closer to the fire. I had to be imagining things. I heard her name spoken and thought that I would recognize her in a photo. I didn't even know her, had only seen her picture in the newspaper. I held up the two photos to compare. In one of them, she was partially hidden in the crowd, but in the other, her face could be seen from the front. Of course that was her! I remembered her wild hairstyle, her long nose, her shapely lips.

She must have been talking or laughing with Vollmer for quite some time. It appeared to have been a very relaxed conversation; at any rate, teacher and student seemed quite comfortable in each other's presence.

Suddenly, unexpectedly, Julian ripped the photos out of my hands. "What are you studying these photos for?! May I, Emra?" He held the printouts above the flames and, not a moment later, dropped them into the fire. "It's probably best if there are as few copies as possible!"

"Did you and Emra...?" I asked. What reason could he have to burn the pictures, if not for fear of my recognizing him?

"Nonsense!" he snapped at me, shaking his head violently. "I have a girlfriend—you! Besides, why would I go to that party? I'm not going to school here, remember?" He seemed seriously offended, snorted, and folded his arms across his chest. "Seriously, you don't trust me at all, huh?"

I didn't reply, and his friends were quiet, too, except for Mickey, who was softly humming to himself and, off-key, sang something along the lines of "please don't fool me."

Why should I trust Julian now?

"But it could be you," I whispered. "You've been here before, and you've got the same pair of shoes."

"Mr. Wende, you are temporarily under arrest. You have no alibi for the time of the incident," Mickey said with a deadly serious look on his face, using his fingers to form the shape of a gun, and pointing it at Julian.

Laura roared with laughter.

Even Julian seemed to think it was funny. "I demand to speak to my lawyer immediately!" he countered in a falsetto voice.

They all laughed, laughed about me.

They probably all knew that the boy in the picture was Julian. Why else had they not mentioned any other names? Why else would they now be raising their glasses to him and shutting me out of their inner circle?

Because I was a stranger, an alien element, someone who had come in from the outside, someone who didn't understand and therefore posed a danger to them. That had to be it. I was a danger to them—and therefore they were a danger to me, too.

I could no longer trust Julian. He had betrayed me, cheated on me, and he would not turn against his friends for my sake; he was with them, and they all stuck together.

I became restless and agitated again. I saw Julian and his friends, laughing and drinking, while my own mouth was completely dry. I saw how—with every drink from the bottle—Dustin's facial expression became more and more strained, and how he kissed Olga, more out of boredom than out of tenderness; he seemed to be more focused on his drinking now. Mickey, on the other hand, didn't need any more; he was already glassy-eyed, and his jokes were so flat and dull that I was horrified to hear Julian laugh at them. He most certainly did not have a whole lot to say in

this circle of friends; he seemed more like a tolerated observer to me, while I, his girlfriend, in their eyes probably had
the same right to exist as the common cockroach.

I sat there, all stiff and tense, and didn't move, while the
evening progressed and the fire went out. None of them
seemed to feel the cold, the moonlight offered enough
light, and their stockpile of alcohol seemed inexhaustible.
They also didn't run out of topics of conversation. They
had returned to Mirko Vollmer, and they were hotly debat-
ing all the possible ways to silence him. That he wouldn't
blow the whistle about the beatings and tell on them to
his dad or even the police—that was something they were
sure of. Unless, well, unless he found someone who would
support him, back him up, confirm his story, act as a
witness.

This remark was enough to make my condition rapidly
deteriorate even further. Vollmer was already in the know.
If Julian made only one wrong remark, their aggression
toward me would flare up again. I found myself fixated on
that thought. I was so tense that I was suddenly barely able
to follow their conversation. Their voices were muffled, as
if I was wrapped in layers of cotton wool. Were they talking
about me? What did they want from me? And why was Julian
prodding me?

"Eva, say something!"

Say what? What does he want me to say? I know nothing.
I don't want to cry. And I don't want them to notice how
lousy I feel.

The fox guy! I try to imagine him sitting beside me,
looking at me. I've had such episodes with him, too: excessive sweating, palpitations, hyperventilation. The fox guy

always stays really, really calm. He sits beside me and looks at me, and nothing is ever as bad as it seems.

"Leave Eva alone already, she very clearly said that she doesn't appreciate Mirko's blackmail campaign!" Chris raised his voice. "We should talk about something else. What about our trip during fall break, for example? We need to start making plans soon!"

They talked about a package deal to Majorca, Spain. Beach and booze. Julian contemplated joining them. Funny, I had no idea. Not that I'm interested either way. In my reality, I'm sitting in the fox guy's office, telling him all of this.

"Emra, it's almost ten. Do you still want me to drive you home? I still can." Chris got up.

"Yes, absolutely. Thanks for doing this. You guys are staying here?"

"Of course," Mickey said. "Or are you cold, Laura? You can come sit on my lap if you're cold."

"I'm coming, too, Chris." Olga kissed Dustin and joined the little group.

"Alright. What about you guys, Julian?"

Please, please say that we want a ride!

"We're going dancing later, right, Dustin?" my boyfriend said.

"Yeah, if you want. Let's wait till Chris gets back; by then it'll be eleven, and we can go down to the Tropic."

"Cool, the Tropic!" Laura inspected her light-colored denim jeans. "I hope I didn't get any grass stains on my pants, I'd have a fit. Dude, do you have any idea how expensive these were?" She nudged Mickey, who didn't seem to notice. Then Laura remembered that there was another girl around here somewhere who was maybe interested in such a topic. But she didn't invite me in on her conversation; she just stared at me, scrutinized me. At that moment, I thought I could downright read her thoughts: "I wouldn't even talk to her if there was no other human being anywhere else on this planet." And I felt miserable, worthless, humiliated, and excluded; I felt ugly. Chris, together with Olga and Emra, went to the car; all my hopes faded away. I was alone. Julian didn't offer me protection, nobody offered me protection, nobody liked me, and not even my imagination helped. I was no longer able to picture the fox guy by my side. It came as no surprise that even he must eventually turn away from someone so despised, so broken. I dug my fingernails deep into my arm, I gasped for air, I wailed because my eyes welled up, and then the food repeated on me and made me nauseous, and right then and there I couldn't take it any longer. I jumped to my feet, saying, "I'm outta here!" and ran off into the darkness.

17

I didn't get very far. Not because Julian called after me that I should stay, that it wasn't safe being out here and running around at night. There was nothing worse for me than being with these people. I would have a major relapse if I stayed with them. Arms raised in front of my face, wiping away tears, pushing aside branches, I bolted through the forest. I didn't stick to the trail that we had come up on, but I was going downhill and that was all that mattered. Most of all I wanted to get down and off this hill, imagined reaching the street and then...yeah, what then? To somehow get to the town, alone, possibly sleep inside a cold, empty railroad station, and then leave without my bags, like a fugitive?

I had absolutely no idea. I was also unfamiliar with the area's geography. I didn't know that there were caves, chasms, slopes, and steep drops. I simply fell.

The ground was suddenly gone from under my feet. My arms flailed in all directions, and a final, crazy thought shot through my mind: So this is the actual goal my vertigo has been aiming for all this time—this moment of falling. And here it was, too unexpected and brief for me to feel fear, terrifying and beautiful all at the same time. Every sense of body, space, and reality was gone, erased, and that in itself was mind-blowing, almost magnificent. At least for a short while.

Then I lay in darkness.

"Eva! Eeeeevaaaa!"

They called my name, again and again. They were above me somewhere; they made twigs snap, cussed, blamed each other.

"If she went down and hurt herself, it's your fault; you were scaring her shitless with all your stupid talk!"

"Oh, you're the one to talk, Julian! You've had too much to drink as usual, and you lost control. That's the only reason she ran off!" That was Dustin.

"Exactly! Why would she be scared of us?" Laura asked. "Nobody should be scared of us, we're totally innocent, we help the weak and the poor!"

"We are the Robin Hoods of Ravenwood Forest!" Mickey roared and, judging by the noise that he made, shook a small tree as if he were a bear.

My eyelids felt like garage doors. Why should I make such an effort to try to keep them open? My head hurt, I was tired, and I just wanted to sleep, fall asleep here on my bed of leaves and clay.

"Eeeva!" Julian's voice sounded seriously worried. "Come back! Please! Eeeeeva! I love you!" How sweet, such drama, almost like a scene from a movie. Who the heck should believe him?!

"Eva! We want to go to the Tropic!" Oh sure, Laura, we'll toast to us and be best friends, and then we'll disappear into the bathroom only to paint our lips conspiratorially and bitch about other girls' legs.

"Eeeva!" They left.

I shouldn't let them go. After all, I needed them, and being in their company was the lesser of two evils.

"Over here!" Alright, alright, I'm getting up. I'd be up already if the world would stop spinning for just a second, if my legs weren't so high up in the air, and if my head wasn't dangling so far below.

There was this exercise I had learned that one time. What was it for again, and did it work? I didn't know the answer, but I was already in the process of doing it, lightly but quickly knocking on a specific area just below my nose using the knuckle of my index finger.

At first, nothing happened; but then I caught a moment during which I was sure to be lying flat on the ground, and I overcame my fear, gathered momentum, and sat up. Shortly afterward I was up and on my feet, heard the voices return, shouted something, and simultaneously grabbed a tree branch so that I was holding on to something. The world stopped spinning. I was able to put things in order: My left wrist was sore, and so was my right knee. Other than that, I seemed to be fine. No blood, no severe pain, no feeling of numbness.

"Eva? Where are you?"

How far down had I fallen? Six, seven feet? Ten? I turned my head upward just a little and immediately regretted it. Good thing I had that tree branch to hold onto.

"Eva? There you are! Thank God!" The beam of a flashlight shone at me from above. "You're alright?" Dustin asked, no longer quite as hostile as before. "Go left, it's a bit tricky to get up here from where you are. The slope gets steepest in about a hundred yards. You'll find stairs there. We'll meet you there."

"Don't worry, there are no more slopes; you're already all the way down. You were super lucky that you fell where you fell. Over there it's much higher up and a lot steeper, over twenty-five feet, it's crazy! I was really worried about you, Evie. You're alright, aren't you?"

"Yeah, Julian, it's okay." I rubbed my face. He must be feeling really guilty, otherwise he wouldn't be talking so much. Whatever! I would get this whole thing over with, would put up a brave front, and behave as dispassionately as possible toward Julian and his friends. I would, if necessary, have a cocktail and then spend the rest of the night with Julian in the mill, but then I'd take the first train home in the morning. Call my parents so that they'd pick me up from the station. Lie to them about my time with Julian, that it had been good but not perfect—that he wasn't my one true love after all. They didn't need to know the truth; that was something I would tell the fox guy, if anyone. Until then I would try to convince myself that, in spite of everything, I had stayed strong, had tried everything.

Holding onto every tree branch like someone seasick on a ship rocking on the high seas, I dragged myself sluggishly and painfully through the beech forest, well below the steep slope. My wrist felt as if it contained splintery chicken bones. My right knee was, beyond a doubt, the hottest part of my body and probably swelling up to the size of a watermelon right about now. My vertigo was stubborn, persistent; but it abated if I focused all of my energy on taking step after step and on the pain in my hand and knee.

At first, I didn't pay any attention to whatever lay to the left or right of my path below the slope, which was, in actual fact, getting steeper and steeper with every step I took. But then I suddenly saw pale colors right beside me on the forest floor. I screamed.

And while I registered what I saw, I couldn't put it into words. The message was received by my brain but was not forwarded to the other parts of my body that discharge emotions, make decisions, create movement. I understood but did not want to understand, a moment of shock stretching to infinity.

So I screamed. As long as I screamed I was alive. If I stopped, I would collapse and lie there a moment later just like her.

My screams were also of very practical use, in that they called Julian and the others over to me in no time at all.

"My God, it's Alina," Laura whispered.

Mickey staggered behind a tree and threw up. Dustin aimed his flashlight at Alina's distorted body, until his arm started shaking uncontrollably and he had to bring it up quickly, helplessly. With a sense of desperation that I did not think he had in him, he roared, "Oh shit, this really sucks!"

Only then did my screams die down, fade into a wail, and then Julian came, put his arms around me, whispered, "Come on, let's get you away from here!" and pulled me away from the sight of the dead girl. Mickey came to join us, wiped his mouth with his hand, and muttered in disbelief, "This can't be real. I'm drunk. Tell me that this isn't real!"

Neither Julian nor I replied. Laura started to cry and leaned against Mickey, who awkwardly grabbed her shoulder while he himself looked as if he needed someone to hold onto. Only Dustin remained by Alina and said, "Julian, call the police!"

My boyfriend needed a long time to fish his cell phone from his pocket, dial nine-one-one, and find some words. Nobody felt bothered by his helpless babbling. That he was able to say anything at all was an achievement in and of itself, of which the rest of us would not have been capable.

Then we stood and waited.

It was eerily quiet. Even Laura was weeping silently, and time seemed to have stopped. This girl lay there. Only a few yards away from us. I thought I could feel the cold rising from her body, her overpowering sweetish smell. But that was impossible. She was not lying as close to me as my granddad had, back then, in the viewing room at the funeral home. I couldn't smell a thing. I also saw practically nothing from where I was standing now. And I most certainly couldn't feel her presence, since Alina wasn't present anymore. She was dead. But that little sensation on my neck, what was that? A twig, a leaf, the wind, what else!

Julian interrupted our shocked silence. "They asked me if it was really her, and if she really was dead. Like, if we're really sure." His breathing came in short, ragged gasps.

Nobody replied. His two friends didn't show any reaction at all; only Laura gave a louder sob to show that she had heard him. I said nothing, even though I was well able to answer the question he had asked: the young girl lying there at the bottom of the steep slope was dead. I had known straightaway, even if I was incapable of explaining why. It was the stiffness of her body, how her limbs were bent at an unnatural angle, the tree branch that had fallen and landed on her back. She must have been lying there for a while, definitely not just since this afternoon. Who knows for how long? Who knows how many wild animals had already sniffed at her body, how many worms and flies…

"Evie, you poor thing, honey, you're whimpering and shaking all over! You don't need to be scared. I'll protect you, I'll hold you, and we're leaving just as soon as the police get here."

My boyfriend. Was that my boyfriend? Was he still by my side, in spite of everything?

"You have to be careful that you don't destroy any evidence!" Laura croaked in the voice of a little girl. "Dustin, you better get away from there! Should we walk to the street? Come on, let's walk down to the street. Please!"

"I can't just leave," Dustin called. "I have to keep an eye on her. You have to go without me."

"We shouldn't split up again," Julian said. "We should stay together. It's safer."

"But there's nothing here we can do…" Laura protested.

"I think we better stick together, too," Mickey muttered, suddenly sober, pulling Laura, who had started wailing, closer to him. "Call the police again, ask them if they're on their way."

"This is Julian Wende again. I, we wanted to ask if you're really coming; we've been waiting and…"

"I want to go hoooome!"

"My friend, yeah, Laura, I don't think she can take it much longer. Actually, none of us can take it much longer. My girlfriend is in a really bad way, and Laura, too… Shock? Don't know, maybe. But you're on your way, right? Okay." Julian lowered his cell phone. "They should be here any minute," he said feebly.

All of us were silent. Laura stopped her siren-like wailing for just a moment, and I was able to hear the voices of the forest again. A gust of wind blew through my hair, and I had to wonder if it blew through Alina's hair now, too, and if it would lift her hair lightly and lower it gently, as it did when she was still alive, when she softly smelled of shampoo and probably combed every little crumb of earth vigorously from her hair. Now, on the other hand...

Thoughts were zigzagging through my mind.

Miniskirt and maxi legs. I hope Laura is racked with guilt. I hope she is suffering in a really bad way. I hope she is really, really sorry about all of this. The two of them had run into each other in the bathroom and had no idea that it would be the last time.

That was Tuesday night, at the school party. While Emra was fooling around and making out with my Julian, Alina had come here. Why? What could she possibly want here? There was nothing out here. Only trees with their long branches, an indifferent moon, sneering stars. She would have been much better off at the party. In the light, inside a house, surrounded by people.

Alina—I hadn't known her and yet would never forget her—was the second dead person I had seen in my life, besides my granddad. Granddad died in a hospital, in the early morning hours before any of his relatives got there, alone. Had Alina been alone, too? Why else did nobody help her when she fell? But did she really fall—or did someone push her?

"Any moment now, Evie. Stay strong! We'll get through this!" said Julian, who could feel that I was starting to tense up again.

"What do you think?" I said slowly and with great effort. "Do you think she killed herself? Was it an accident, or... or..."

Julian cleared his throat. Laura was having something like the cry-hiccups.

"Dude, if that wasn't an accident they better catch this guy and...and..." Mickey growled like an angry dog, clenched his fists, and gritted his teeth. "If I find out who it was, I—"

"What then?" Dustin interrupted. "Do you want us to beat him up, like Mirko?"

Whereupon Mickey stopped talking, and even I noticed that he was talking utter nonsense, despite my being in shock.

After all, we weren't investigators or detectives, and we had no idea who hurt this girl, if that's what really happened. Some of us did know her and were able to confirm seeing her at her very last party. But that was really it. For all intents and purposes, we had found her, by accident, simply because I had tripped over her dead body.

Good lord, what a terrible thought! It was just as well that I hadn't really memorized that image! By now, practically all I remembered was that Alina wasn't naked, that she was wearing a blue denim skirt and a burgundy-colored jacket. I hadn't really seen anything else. Except her hand. If that light-colored, little something bathed in moonlight and resting on a bed of leaves really was her hand. I narrowed my eyes to wipe out the image of the hand, but it was no use. I looked down at my own soft hand, caressed it awkwardly, saying, "No, no, it's not true, it's not so bad..." and on and on, and I only noticed that tears were coming down my cheeks in rivers when Julian used a tissue to wipe them away.

18

Finally, lights appeared and came closer; the police had arrived.

They took us away from the place where we had found the body, took us to the forest road where their cars were parked, asked us many questions, and tried their best to comfort and reassure us. I couldn't say much, held on to a cup of stale tea while sitting beside Laura in the police van, and made every effort to comprehend why I had left the picnic ground and had so blindly run off.

"My boyfriend, Julian, and I had a fight," I explained. "I think he's seeing someone else."

That was only half the truth, of course. I didn't mention the school party, Mirko's blackmail attempts, the group of friends' revenge. When the gray-haired police officer with the beard, the one I had met that afternoon, recognized me and casually asked me if I wanted to add anything about the fight I had witnessed, I declined.

"Well, this sure is the least of our worries right now." He nodded and looked at me compassionately, as if thinking that I was having the worst of luck during my vacation. "Should you remember something else—"

"I won't."

"Stop running through the forest on your own like a chicken with its head cut off! We don't know what we're dealing with here, I told you that earlier today."

"I know. I will remember from now on, I promise."

"Good." He smiled encouragingly and left.

They had finished questioning us for now. After all, we had "only" found Alina, hadn't touched anything, hadn't moved or changed anything. We now waited to be officially allowed to leave. In that unobserved moment, Laura pinched me and said quietly, "You really *are* dependable. Thanks. Besides, our little problem really has nothing to do with this thing here."

"No, it doesn't," I replied. Because I absolutely believed it.

A police patrol car took Julian and me back to the mill, and another car took the other three back into town since Laura didn't dare to drive by herself. When we were about halfway, we met Chris in his off-roader; the police briefly questioned him and then sent him on his way.

"So much for our vacation," Julian said in a flat voice as we stood in front of the main door to the apartment with the police car leaving.

"Yeah well," I murmured, "I wasn't in the best of moods anyway, but..." Now that everyone had left, that no more questions remained to be answered, that nothing was left to be done—now reality started sinking in. A girl had died, and I could have died, too. I already risked my life on that first evening, when I walked through the forest so carelessly; but today I had an accident and fell in a similar spot to where Alina herself had fallen to her death. And, for just a split second, I even thought that falling was beautiful. This brought tears to my eyes. I felt so guilty. What the heck was I thinking?

Julian put his arm around me, unlocked the front door, and gently shoved me inside.

"I think we both need a rest. And here I was thinking that we'd be happy, that we'd get to spend some alone-time together..."

Suddenly he started to cry. He must have been holding back the tears this whole entire time, but now he couldn't hold them back any longer. He buried his face in his hands, turned his back to me, leaned against the door with his forehead.

"I am so, so sorry. That I lied to you, that nothing is going well, and now this to top it all off." He took a deep breath and blew his nose. "It's just too much! And why Alina, of all people? I mean, I didn't know her well, but I saw her a couple of times; she even came to the mill a few times for something or other. She was a little crazy, but she was super nice, somehow exactly like you."

"Like me?" I asked with a start.

"Yeah, no, not the way she looked, but her character, you know? She was full of energy and had so many dreams and talents, but she didn't project it to the outside, like Laura does for example. No, she was quiet for the most part, and withdrawn and ambitious; yeah, ambitious, like you, and sometimes it just kind of flared up, like, totally unexpected. It all sounds very complicated and confusing, and I don't know how else to explain it, but for example, she was more than chubby, she was quite fat, yeah, and she still looked really great and sexy, despite her enormous backside! Laura is nothing compared to her! And then sometimes, Alina would tell you a great story and wow you with her paintings; she could really electrify you. No wonder Laura didn't like her. Alina lived a much more intensive life. So what if she ran away once or twice, or if she smoked pot—who cares? Alina was interesting, right, and not so easy to figure out. Sometimes she was even pretty shy, cautious somehow. I'm not sure, but I think she was keeping a lot of secrets. Yeah, she was very special, a very special person. Just like you."

I couldn't bear the thought of it.

"Oh please, don't say that!"

"But it's true. I bet she kept a diary, too, and if someone told her, 'Don't go through the forest!' she was all the more determined to go."

"Julian, please, stop it!" I leaned my forehead against his back and wrapped my arms around his belly. My tears soaked through his sweatshirt, and when he turned around they mixed with his.

We had a very rough night and hardly slept at all. The night seemed endless, dark, and menacing. Even the short walk to the bathroom, where I needed to drag myself several times, seemed doomed and dangerous to me. I was glad that Julian was awake when I returned to bed and put his arm around me. It gave me a certain sense of security. He seemed to feel the same way because he was a lot more affectionate than he had been in a long while.

"You'll stay with me, won't you?" he whispered in the early morning hours. "You'll stay here today like we planned, right, Eva?"

I muttered something affirmative, even though I would much rather be in the big city—surrounded by people—than all alone out here in the great outdoors. Besides, the right moment to leave was gone anyway. Because it was I who had found Alina, I couldn't just disappear. I wasn't sure why, though. Because I wanted to buy some flowers and put them down at the scene of the accident? Because the police had stated that there might be further questions, and Julian responded that we'd be in the mill until Sunday noon? Because there might be something that I wanted to say regarding Alina's case after all?

I tossed and I turned. The red LED digits on the radio alarm clock showed 4:38 a.m. On her finger, Alina had been wearing a ring with a red stone. It had twinkled in the moonlight. In fact, it was the twinkle of that stone that I had seen first. I groaned. Julian pulled me closer to his warm body.

"Try to get some sleep."

Sleep...

In my half-dream I'm running through the forest, I'm falling down several times, I'm plummeting down the slope. The slope gets steeper and steeper, until I get to the spot where Alina is lying. I can see her hand.

She's waving at me.

19

When I got up it was almost noon. Sleep had overcome me in the end, but it hadn't refreshed me. I was tense all over, had a headache, a sprained wrist, a swollen knee, and I was in a mood befitting the gray, depressing weather.

Julian was still asleep. I let him sleep, traipsed barefoot into the bathroom, and then downstairs into the kitchen. The floor tiles were cold. I couldn't find aspirin or anything similar in the cupboards. I made coffee; yawned; rubbed one naked foot against my leg, then the other; pushed ready-to-bake breakfast rolls into the oven; put Julian's ice bag on my wrist; turned the radio on, hoping to hear something about the investigation regarding Alina's case; dialed my parents' home number but didn't reach anyone. While it was perfectly understandable that I was sad, why would I feel so lonely when looking out the window?

Because, you see, I wasn't alone. Bernd Vollmer was walking past my window. Without looking up, he unlocked the door to the gear house and disappeared inside the garage. I wondered whether he received the daily local newspaper and already knew about Alina. I was standing there, buried in thought, when his son showed up, too. Mirko Vollmer was carrying a grubby school backpack over his shoulders and wore the same beige-orange sports jacket that he had worn Thursday night. The tear on his elbow was provisionally stitched up. In contrast to his dad, Mirko had dark, curly hair; he didn't look anything like him. He didn't follow him into the garage but waited outside, like a bored child, hands buried in his jeans pockets, shoulders pulled up almost all the way to his ears, listlessly kicking something in front of him. Then he noticed that he was being watched, stopped—and our eyes met.

They had beaten him up good, no doubt about that. His face looked pitiful. He skewed his mouth. Was that supposed to be a grin, a hello? Surely he had seen me from his window yesterday and knew who I was: the girl who had witnessed how he was beaten up. My guilty conscience raised its ugly head again; at the same time, anger rose inside of me when I remembered how much trouble he had caused for Emra.

And not only for Emra, I corrected myself, but also for the boy who was with her in the picture. If I wanted to find out if it was Julian, this was the right moment. More to the point: the answer to this question would distract me from the image of poor, dead Alina that was, unchanged, still haunting my mind. Mirko and I kept looking at each other. I was of two extremely conflicting minds. Curiosity won. I opened the window. "Hi."

He narrowed his eyes, took a step back.

"I know where you got that from." I pointed to his black eye and the tear in his jacket. "That was very unfair of them, and I'm sorry. But I also know why they did it."

Didn't that come out just right? The fox guy couldn't have said it better! For a moment, I thought about how awesome I was, and then I saw Bernd coming from the garage and heard Mirko reply, "I don't know what you're talking about. I didn't do anything to anyone! I was attacked for absolutely no reason! The assholes who did this should actually be reported to the police!"

"So Julian does have something to do with it, does he?" Bernd Vollmer asked. "Well, I've been wanting to call his parents anyway."

"You know as well as I do that Julian wasn't there," I called out.

That man unnerved me. He was pretty good-looking in this short-sleeved shirt that he was wearing despite the rainy weather, with his tanned skin and just the right amount of designer stubble—a little bit like a certain movie star whose name I could not remember. But that disdainful look on his face! I felt naked and inferior under his gaze, and not just because I hadn't combed my hair and was wearing one of Julian's oversized sweatshirts over my nightgown.

I pointed at Mirko.

"You took pictures of Emra and tried to use them to blackmail her!" It wasn't very graceful and it was a sign of weakness to get so worked up, but Vollmer's who-the-heck-do-you-think-you-are look and Mirko's incessant head-shaking put me on the spot and unwittingly made me side with Emra and her group of friends. "I saw the photos with my own eyes before we burned them! Don't tell me you don't know how Muslims might react if you wave those kinds of pictures of their daughter under their noses!"

The three snapshots materialized before my eyes again: crowded, smoke-filled, school party atmosphere. Lots of people dancing, talking, laughing, drinking, and partying without taking notice that they were being photographed. In the foreground, Emra and that mysterious stranger—my boyfriend?

To be honest, of course, I didn't care at all about justice for Emra; I only cared about my relationship with Julian.

Mirko either didn't realize what I was getting at, or he really didn't want to budge. He shook his head in resignation. "Whatever it is they're telling you, be careful what you believe. Shaky half-truths make up half of everything people say. Let me tell you how it was for me, okay? I took pictures, that's right. I printed three of them afterward, but only this one time, and only those three. Emra grabbed them from me right away; she was behaving like a crazy person. I guess she and her lover are regretting how much they were living it up at the party. They got drunk, they were making out, they were fooling around in public. For her, not exactly pure and chaste like a virgin or whatever; and for him... But that's their problem, not mine. 'I'll give you the photos,' I told her, 'so you can paste them in your family album. Your dad will be thrilled, I'm sure.' That was it. Just an ironic comment, nothing else."

Vollmer listened in, frowning.

"I didn't know anything about this. Well, you can tell me the whole story again in a minute. You're nothing but trouble, you know—the photos, that thing with those friends..." He muttered a few more incomprehensible things under his breath and then grabbed his son's arm. "Come on, let's go!"

"If that's true, then it was a misunderstanding," I called after Mirko. "Emra really thinks that you have it in for her. But I can talk to her. If I see you deleting the files from your computer, and if you give me the printed photos and the cell phone, too, then she'll know that you weren't trying to blackmail her. Then we can fix this whole thing; she can give you back your cell phone as soon as she's deleted everything, and—"

"Hold on!" Bernd Vollmer suddenly barked. "My son does not need to justify his behavior or defend himself in any way, shape, or form! Your friends can count themselves lucky that Mirko is not pressing charges for physical assault. Because if I were him, I would."

"But—"

"So, if I understand correctly, you're having trouble with your boyfriend, Julian? Is that him in the photos? Mirko, I don't think you need to spare her feelings out of some unnecessary consideration; I think you can be very clear with her."

Mirko didn't say a word. To spare me or to provoke me?

Or because his dad, in pointing a finger at Julian, had just voiced a suspicion he had made up on the spot to keep me in check?

"Is that why you're getting so involved in things that are of no, and I mean absolutely no, concern to you, young lady?"

I wanted to say something, but Vollmer was just getting started. "Are you always this involved when it comes to the well-being of the weak and misfortunate, or are there ever moments when you lose your noble, selfless courage?"

Darn it, this wasn't going too well! I had to pull the emergency brake. "But this *does* concern me. I got involved in the whole thing by accident, and I also happened to find Alina yesterday. Besides, these photos have an additional meaning, Mirko: They show Alina in the background. And you, too, Mr. Vollmer."

Bingo! Even though I was clearly and selfishly swapping apples for oranges, my words were having an effect. Vollmer's eyes widened in horror; Mirko scowled at me.

"Alina?" Vollmer exclaimed. "What, why? What about her?"

"She's dead. She fell down a steep, rocky slope. Out in the woods, by the castle ruins."

"Good God!" Vollmer stared at me in horror for a moment, and then he ran into the garage.

Mirko and I followed him with our eyes, in silence. I was embarrassed—because I had used this tragic event for my own petty jealousy issues and had pulled it from my sleeve like an ace, without any consideration. Darn you, Eva! A girl is dead, and all you can think about is that stupid make-out session!

This sudden epiphany pulled the rug from under me. I saw myself back in the forest, falling, plummeting, and then seeing her there, a corpse.

"That's horrible," I heard Mirko say from very far away. And a little later: "You found her. That's harsh. Hey, are you alright?"

"Low blood pressure."

"You're feeling shaky, like vertigo?" he asked empathically and intelligently at the same time.

"Shaky half-truths make up half of everything people say," I quoted him laconically.

"Love the other half, and real truths—death."

"Wow, very deep," I muttered. "Who said it?"

"I did. I'm going to be a philosopher one day."

"Ah." The spinning subsided. I saw Mirko standing there, pouting, puppy-eyed. He looked mischievous, but clumsy and awkward all at the same time.

"It must have been awful to find her like that." He nod-ded to himself. "I barely knew her, and she probably didn't like me any more than any of my classmates, but I still feel shocked by her death. This really sucks. Do we know how it happened? Was it an accident?"

I shrugged my shoulders.

Mirko pulled a face again. "They're investigating now, are they?" he asked quietly.

"I think so." I didn't want to think too much about the police work you typically see on a TV crime show: contacting the next of kin, questioning, securing evidence, pathology.

Vollmer reversed his car from the garage, stopped with the engine running, and pulled down the driver's window.

"I have to ask again: So you really did find Alina Westkamp dead in the forest by the castle ruins?"

"Yes," I replied, and you couldn't help but notice how blotchy Bernd Vollmer's face was. You could almost think that he'd been crying about the high school student's death in quiet sympathy. But I was probably imagining things.

"Do we already know how and why…?" Vollmer broke off, shook his head, looked away.

"Probably an accident, Daddy," Mirko speculated.

"The police didn't tell us. The only thing I know is that, in your photos—"

Vollmer honked his horn.

"To hell with those photos! Mirko! You coming?!"

Mirko turned around to his dad, then back to me. Slowly and well-rehearsed, as if testifying in court, he said, "I would really like to help whoever, but unfortunately I immediately deleted the three photos from the school com-puter on Thursday morning, just like your friends asked me to. I lost the cell phone when your friends were chasing me afterward. There are no files on my own computer because I didn't get a chance to look at the pictures on Wednesday. So, there are no other photos."

"Oh, come on, don't give me that!"

"Have you ever been threatened and chased by people who wanted to beat you up? Have you ever done something somebody else forced you to do? Have you ever lost anything? Have you ever been scared?"

I opened my mouth, but Vollmer beat me to it.

"Enough already!" He stepped on the gas, and Mirko hurried to get into the car.

"Bye!" he said.

I followed them with my eyes as they left. In the silence they left behind, I thought I could hear my own heartbeat. I was so upset that I had to sit down on the floor tiles for a while. I had been sweating and was extremely tense; at any rate, the pain inside my head had reached unheard-of levels. Worn out and exhausted, I took the ice bag that had fallen to the floor and pressed it against my forehead. I was none the wiser.

I sat there for quite a while. I thought about Alina and let my tears flow freely until I was so cold that I had to force myself to get up, make some breakfast, and carry it upstairs to Julian. Fortunately, he was fast asleep and hadn't taken any notice of my conversation with the Vollmers. I decided to keep it that way.

28

We had breakfast in bed—not happy, boisterous, and loving this time, but full of suspicion, without appetite, and without saying much. Every sentence we started was about Alina, and we always broke off mid-sentence. "Did you see how…?" "Do you think she could have been saved if…?" "If her parents had called the police sooner, maybe…" "If only she'd had her cell phone on her, maybe that could have been located by satellite…" "If only the police had searched there instead of the area around the school, then…"

"Then that wouldn't have changed anything, except for the fact that it wouldn't have been us finding her." Julian finished at least that last sentence and disappeared into the bathroom. I tried to pass the time by picking up my new journal and jotting down a few notes about all the terrifying events that had happened to me since arriving in Munkelbach. I decided to take a pass on reliving my feelings in their entirety; I would only be able to do so after a certain amount of time had passed. And so I just listed the facts:

–Tuesday night: Emra and Julian make out (?), Mirko takes their picture, Alina and Bernd can be seen in the background of the picture, Alina disappears

–Later, Mirko is blackmailing Emra (misunderstanding?)
–Thursday night: Mirko is beaten up, tells me he doesn't have his cell phone on him (?), tells me he lost it (?), tells me...

What was it that Mirko told me?

Right at that moment, Julian emerged from the bathroom.

"So, how do you like your new diary? You don't miss your old one anymore?"

I looked out the window. It had started to rain. Wherever my diary might be lying out there—the ink would have started to run by now anyway.

"What are you writing about, anyways?" He sat down on the bed, trying to catch a glimpse of the few handwritten lines.

"Just some bullet points," I replied and quietly added in my head: very little text and a lot of question marks.

"I see." Julian cocked his head to one side, grinned. "Can I read it?"

"No." I was getting annoyed. What the heck was he thinking? "Journals are very personal. They lose all meaning if other people read them."

"Just the first page? Please?" He grabbed my feet, tickled them. "Or are you keeping secrets from me?"

"Oh, I think it's *you* who's keeping secrets from *me*," I corrected him.

"Yeah." Julian sighed, let go of my feet, and fell back on the bed. "I know. The fake foot injury, that thing with my friends...I had no choice, Eva. I'm sorry."

"And what about Emra?"

"Emra? Whatever!" He made a dismissive gesture, stood up.

"Was that you in the photo? I want to know!"

"No, goddammit! Jeez, is that the only thing you can ever think about? As if we didn't have any worse or even more important issues to worry about!" Julian blushed and darted from the bedroom.

I remained sitting on the bed, sad. I didn't believe him, that was it. Even if nobody would confirm my suspicions and even if I couldn't be 100 percent sure, my instincts were speaking a very clear language: Julian was lying.

We might as well end it right here and now. That's what I wanted anyway, wasn't it? Why wouldn't I just go home to my parents?

Because of Alina? Was it sensationalism? Compassion? Ah, whatever, I didn't know! Like it mattered anyway.

That, I remembered, was what Mirko had said in the forest two days ago. "Like it matters anyway." I jotted it down on the next page. And then I added: *Shaky half-truths make up half of everything people say, love the other half, and real truths— death.* I kind of liked that saying.

Today's "recreational activity" consisted of a drive to the shopping mall a couple of miles away. With a constant stream of light and breezy music, and surrounded by scores of people, I felt much better than within the oppressive atmosphere of the mill. But maybe that was also thanks to the two aspirin tablets I had taken in the meantime.

As soon as we arrived in the mall, I noticed someone waving at us: Chris.

"Hey, you two! You're not doing so well either, huh?"

"You can say that again," Julian growled.

"I bet. Boy, am I glad that I didn't get to see her. Dustin said you spotted her first, Eva?"

I sighed.

"There's a big report in the newspaper. It was pretty hard just to read it. But then to also experience it first-hand—wow, you poor thing!" Chris was nice and seemed able to empathize.

Julian made a somewhat friendlier face, took my hand.

"Are you going to the Tropic tonight? Maybe we'll come, too."

"I think so," Chris replied and stepped closer to me in a good-natured kind of way. "Are you even up for spending any more time with us?"

"Uh…" What could I say? That I wasn't exactly thrilled to see Laura, Mickey, and Dustin again? We had a deal that Julian and I would be spending time together, just the two of us. On the other hand, we'd already dropped our lines of communication, so to speak, and our relationship had suffered to such a degree that a distraction would probably do us good. Besides, dealing with a shock such as the one we experienced last night was probably better done in a group; and one of the reasons why I had stayed this morning—and I suddenly realized this—was Alina's death. I had found her; according to Julian, she had been quite similar to me; I had been preoccupied with her so much; and I really wanted to find out what happened to her. Just to go back home and pretend nothing happened or as if her fate didn't mean anything to me—that was not an option.

And so I added, "It's alright. I like dancing."

"Me too." Chris seemed really happy about that. "It really helps when you can dance your stress and worries away." He glanced at Julian, who had stopped by a store window to check out some special offers on sneakers, lowered his voice, and said, seemingly offhandedly, "Listen, do you know now who Emra was with that night?"

"Why?"

"Just because. Just thought you wanted to know."

Julian caught up to us again, and suddenly Chris was in a hurry. "I'm off. Are you guys staying?"

Julian nodded. "We only got here a few minutes ago."

"Okay, have fun shopping. See you tonight. Can't wait."

"Is something going on?" Julian asked after Chris had left.

"Nah," I said.

"Okay, then. Do you want to get a cappuccino?"

"Sure, why not."

We sat down in a café overlooking the parking lot and of course reached for the newspaper right away.

The *Munkelbach Gazette* reported on the death on page one. "Cheerful teenagers in a party mood" had allegedly found the girl, "were completely distraught at this time" and "were receiving psychological counseling."

"What a load of crap!" Julian grumbled. "Psychological counseling—who came up with that nonsense?!"

"Would it be so bad?" I asked, quickly and pretty covertly.

"No, I guess not, but…" He tapped his forehead. "First of all, nobody's offered us any counseling. And second of all, I wouldn't accept it even if they offered it to me." He shook his head, drank from his coffee. "What's wrong? You have a funny look on your face. Did Chris say something?"

"Nothing I didn't already know," I countered. One thing was certain: it was a good idea that I hadn't told Julian about my visits to the fox guy. Julian was nice enough, but not only was he extremely erratic and unfaithful, he was also nothing special. It would be painful to end it, but I would survive.

I turned away from him, folded my arms across my chest, and looked at the parking lot. At some point in the future, I thought, our whole entire planet will be one big parking lot. And as terrible and heartbreaking as that was, I really couldn't care less right now.

"Everything alright, Evie?"

"Will you stop calling me *Evie*! I don't even know why I've been putting up with it this whole time. It's such a stupid name! I don't want to hear it anymore!"

"Alright, alright!" Julian raised his hands. "I won't say it anymore." He folded his arms across his chest. "I won't say anything anymore!"

"Oh, don't pretend to be all upset. I'm not upset."

"Do you even have a reason to be upset?" he asked but didn't wait for me to answer. Instead, he buried his head in his arms and said, full of self-pity, "What a screwed-up weekend!"

I sighed, took hold of the newspaper again, and stared at the photos of Alina, her laughter, and her cheerful eyes. She was full of energy, Julian had said. You could tell by her eyes—even in those badly printed newspaper photos.

"I feel like crying, too," Julian said quietly, handed me a tissue, and moved closer. "But I don't know anything else about Alina except for what I told you yesterday. She would have graduated from high school next year, so she wasn't in the same class as my friends. I think only Laura knew her a little better because they were both in the same dance class together." He leaned his head against mine. "I don't know a lot of people here in Munkelbach outside my circle of friends, even though I feel so at home here."

"How did you first meet your friends, anyway?" I asked. I wasn't sure if I was even interested in this, but I wanted to talk about something, anything.

"It was Sneaky's birthday, and he invited them."

"You mean Mirko?"

"Sneaky, right. Have you ever noticed how he walks? He creeps around without making a sound, always shows up out of the blue, and then stares at you like an idiot. Alright, so it was summer break, we were maybe eight or nine years old, and we were playing Robin Hood out in the forest. Mirko wasn't one of the thieves; I wasn't either, at least not at first. Which I thought was stupid, because first, I really rather wanted to be a thief, and second, because they were in the majority. There were two girls there besides Mirko and me, I forgot their names; they were playing knights. They didn't want to play, didn't want to get dirty; they were bored the whole entire time, and they were just sitting in our castle, whispering and saying how they were princesses and how they didn't need to do anything except look pretty, and so pretty soon they got themselves kidnapped by the thieves."

The summer forest appeared before my mind's eye, with its big, shadowy canopy, birds singing, and the cool, gurgling stream. I imagined how I myself would be romping around in there, listening to the calls of all the other kids, and feeling the prickling of stinging nettles on my bare legs.

"At first, Mirko and I were fighting hopeless battles against the thieves. I had no other choice, I didn't know the gang, only knew him. But I realized pretty quickly that they didn't like him. To be honest, I'm not even sure why he invited them in the first place."

"Maybe he was thinking that it would get better?"

"Nah, I think his mother made him."

"I haven't seen her at all. Are Mirko's parents divorced?"

"No, Katja died of cancer when she was very young. She was really nice. She was Mom's best friend. It was thanks to her that we got the vacation apartment. My parents were pretty hard hit when she died. For a while, they didn't even want to come here anymore. Especially my mom found it very hard to get over it."

"And Mirko, too, right...?"

"Oh, come on, forget about Sneaky. I've got no pity for him at all."

"Julian!"

"No, *Eva!* He's a fraud, believe me. Even back then, when we were playing Robin Hood, he came up with this nasty plan of how we could still win against the thieves. He wanted me to lure two of them into the castle—we only had a rain shelter, while the thieves had of course occupied the very awesome Devil's Gorge—allegedly to make them a peace offering. But Mirko filled a basket with pebbles without my knowledge, climbed a tree, and started throwing stones at them from a safe distance."

"Quite a rough game, then, huh!" I said, in true Dr. Fuchs style. "Did anybody get hurt?"

"No, it was only small pebbles, and lots of little twigs, and lumps of dirt. It was never really dangerous, but still...

Okay, so they did tease Sneaky and on his birthday of all days, but… Whatever, I don't know; at any rate, I didn't like it, and when the thieves were running away, I beat it, too."

I smirked.

"A defector, so to speak."

"Exactly." Julian cuddled up to me. "Mirko, of course, resented me for it. I did tell him that I would have been taken prisoner just like the two girls, but he wouldn't have any of it. For a good while afterward, we still played together on occasion, but as I got older and was able to ride my own bike into town and to the public pool, I would only ever meet up with the guys who had played the thieves. If you ask me, I don't think he has ever forgiven me for letting him down and for leaving him behind back then. It's funny. Even though I don't live here, I've got more friends than he does. Chris, for example, asked me if I wanted to train with his handball squad once in a while, and Dustin, who's quite good on the drums, wants to get a band together and asked me to join."

"Well, I guess you're popular." I clearly recalled the single most important question that had plagued me when I met Julian for the first time: Why would an athletic, good-looking, self-confident guy who was also into music be interested in me of all people? Someone like him would always be part of the gang of heroic thieves; part of those who were better looking, more skilled, and smarter; those who maybe weren't better at most things than the average person but were brave enough to be the first ones to try. I was able to relate to what Mirko must have been going through when Julian ran away with the other kids—all of whom were, after all, his guests at his own birthday party.

Julian had already forgotten all about it.

"I haven't even unpacked my saxophone yet. Do we want to jam a little? The weather is perfect for it. Laura is the one who absolutely wants to be our singer if we really do get a band together, but you have a much better voice, and—"

"Oh, I'm not sure." I got up. The fact that I had stayed and would go to the Tropic with them tonight did not mean that I had forgiven Julian for his lies and for that business with Emra—and, most importantly, it didn't mean that I was planning on coming here ever again. Besides, Laura was the one with the biggest mouth, so she *would* sing, whether or not she was talented. You really got the short end of the stick if you were someone like Mirko or me.

Julian paid, put his arm through mine, and strolled with me across the rain-drenched parking lot.

"Hey, the weather is picking up! We're so lucky! When it's pouring rain we can forget about riding the bike."

We got on. Before he started the engine, he pushed his helmet up one more time and pressed a kiss against my lips. Shortly afterward, we parked the Enduro dirt bike inside the garage beside Vollmer's jeep. We were on dry ground as we walked over to the apartment.

21

The white envelope was lying on the doormat. My first, unassuming thought was: Oh, look, the postal service comes all the way out here. Now that's what I call service! Then I noticed that there was no postal stamp on the envelope. I started getting a bad feeling instantly.

"Whoops? What's that?" Julian bent down, read the name on the envelope that was written in block letters. "For you." He gave me a quizzical look.

"But nobody here knows me!" I countered. That sounded idiotic, like I was defending myself.

"It says here: *For Eva in the mill.* Hmm, now I'm curious! Maybe you got yourself a secret admirer?"

"Nonsense!" Nervously I ripped open the envelope.

Julian strained his neck trying to see.

"Who knows? Chris maybe? I think he likes you."

"Oh, come on, stop it." I unfolded the two A4 letter-size sheets.

For a moment we both stared at the top page, read the lines over and over, which were also written in block letters.

Then Julian started yelling: "What the hell?!"

I was unable to respond. The dark block letters were twisting and winding before my eyes, like a snake; they also made the ground beneath my feet tremble with a sense of foreboding. *I'm in the mood to broadcast these confessions all over town. Will you be staying long?* A threat letter!

"Let me see!" Julian pulled the second piece of paper from my hands, and I recognized the writing before he even started to read and before I heard the apparently photocopied text from his mouth:

"During one of our talks, when I was in such a state, I glanced over at him. As usual, he wouldn't take his eyes off me for even one second. I was fighting back my tears, and he kept looking at me in all seriousness, mouth open, eyes narrowed, highly concentrated. I felt imprisoned, like an insect on a display board, helpless and wide open before him, the fox guy, like I had been skinned, X-rayed, and dissected. This was the moment I had feared most of all since the beginning. I held his gaze, though, because in my heart I knew that he meant me no harm, and because I trusted the fox guy. And so I began to talk in my frail, quiet voice, as if I weren't strong enough to add more volume to my own voice. While I was talking, I held on to my shaking knees, and the fox guy was there the entire time, but I didn't really take notice of him anymore then, he didn't interrupt me either. He waited longer and asked a question every now and again, very nicely, very gently, and that's true, too. I told him my worst secret. I told him that—

Before I went home, he told me that he would always be there for me. What an unbelievably corny, shamelessly phony phrase, but it just felt so good. I hate to admit it, but I need him. Sometimes I need my fox guy as much as I need my Julian."

Julian exhaled noisily through his nose.

"What is this?"

My voice was as faint and as squeaky as a mouse's.

"My journal."

"Yeah, that's what I thought!" he shrieked. "But what's written right *there*?" He pointed at the gap in the lower part of the text. The sentence that ushered in the most crucial passages had been cut off in the middle during the photocopying process—and it was obvious that something was missing, even without reading it first. "What kind of weird stuff are you writing about in your diary? What fox guy? What secrets? What am I, stupid and clueless?"

"Julian, I can explain. It's all totally harmless."

He wasn't even listening to me.

"I thought you were writing about stuff like whether you had oatmeal or eggs for breakfast! That's what *I* would consider harmless! Jeez, now I get it why you wanted that thing back so desperately! You've got another boyfriend. That's it, isn't it?!"

"No, no, you have it completely wrong!" I screamed, close to tears. "The fox guy is a kind of *confidant*, you know, someone I trust, and before our vacation I already decided to tell you all about him. But we haven't had a single second alone together!" That was exactly it, I thought: This vacation was the trip from hell! My suddenly rising anger was fueling my strength. "The craziest things keep happening, one after the other, and now someone is even *blackmailing* me using my journal—and you've got nothing better to do but to blame me!" I saw him cringe. That's right! What I said was true. "You're totally off base! Do you have any idea how scary this is to me?" I smacked the piece of paper in his hands. "Scary, Julian! And I think I'm 100 percent entitled to be scared." My tears were flowing freely now, which irritated me, but at the same time I could feel how exhausted and shocked I was. I bolted up the stairs, threw myself—stomach first—onto the bed, buried my face in the pillow, and sobbed uncontrollably.

It took a while for Julian to follow me, sit down on the edge of the bed, put a hand on my shoulder, and say, "I'm sorry. You can of course write whatever you want in your diary."

I didn't reply; it would have come out more like a sob anyway. Julian had no idea how bad it was that a stranger—and someone meaning me harm on top of it all—was reading my journal. It was as if he was gaining entry into my soul. It had taken me long enough to allow the fox guy—whom I had learned to trust completely in the meantime—insight into my secret, innermost thoughts and feelings. And now this! Now this stranger was forcing his way in! I instinctively ruled out a female threat-letter writer—even Laura would respect the intimacy and privacy of a personal journal. This was soul rape! Mean and atrocious! I wanted to bawl my eyes out, was sick to my stomach, wanted to scream so loud that it would shatter the world to pieces!

Several minutes passed. Julian was helpless, didn't say anything. Finally—I calmed down somewhat—he handed me a tissue, and I blew my nose, slipped off my shoes, and sat up in bed with my back up against the softly shaking wall.

My boyfriend followed suit.

"Who do you think would do that?" he asked, as matter-of-factly as he could. "He or she must definitely have a very good reason. To photocopy something, to write a note using only anonymous block letters—that doesn't just happen out of the blue, that's not something you would do for a little kid's prank."

"Nope, surely not. Somebody really wants to mess with me. They want me to disappear." I started shivering as soon as I said it. I reached for the blanket and pulled it up and over my jeans, all the way up to my chin.

Julian put his arm around me.

"But who, and why? My friends know that you won't rat them out! And Dustin and Mickey, for example, they don't even have a driver's license, so it would be extremely difficult for them to even come here by themselves; plus, nobody would be using their bicycle in this weather! Of course, Laura could have driven them here, or Chris…but we only just saw Chris a little while ago!"

"I really can't imagine Chris doing this," I threw in.

"You like him, right? I noticed." He sounded sad and irritated at the same time.

"That's nonsense!" I hissed and rolled my eyes.

"But it could have been Chris," Julian insisted and counted the number of arguments on the fingers of his hand. "He has a car, and he knew that we'd be staying at the mall so that he could make it to the mill unnoticed. Also, he wasn't there yesterday when we found Alina, and so he's not as rattled as we all are."

I opened my mouth to instinctively defend Chris, but I stopped myself just in time. For starters, I didn't want to irritate Julian any further, and secondly, Chris's last remark floated into my mind again. Why would he start talking to me about Emra's make-out session? Did he want to stir up any doubts I had about Julian being faithful (or not), did he want to open my eyes, or was he just in the business of making snide remarks? What business was it of his, anyway?

"The thing that bothers me most is this: it can really only be someone from my circle of friends!" Julian said. "Nobody else would have a motive! Nobody here knows you! Or have you been to Munkelbach before?"

I shook my head.

"Did something happen on the train?"

I recalled the endless train ride, and that girl with all the piercings. How long ago that was! Not even two days, and it seemed like weeks to me.

"No," I said vehemently. "No, I think I only lost the diary in the forest."

"The only question is, how did my friends get ahold of the diary?"

"Before they drove off and left Mirko lying there, one of them leaned out the window. I don't remember what exactly he said, but it was something along the lines that he maybe wanted to come back later to check if his victim had survived the beatings."

Julian pulled a face.

"Was it really that bad? Seriously? I called Dustin on Thursday night, while you were in the shower, and he told me that they were being pretty soft."

I scoffed at him. Ultimately, I detested every single one of them: self-righteous Dustin, dumb and shallow Mickey, and Laura, who was such a cow.

"Who was it who said that they wanted to come back?" Julian asked.

"*He* wanted to come back, by himself. Maybe, he said."

"So who was it?"

"The driver: Chris."

"Ah."

"Yep." I felt how, against my will, I was growing more and more suspicious of the only person in the group of friends whom I liked. Was there no other possible suspect besides Chris? What about Bernd Vollmer and his son? Mirko seemed to be the scapegoat for everything; he was the group's fleabag, so to speak. If I mentioned his name, Julian would agree with me right away. I recalled Mirko's smashed face. Did I really need to jump on the bandwagon along with everyone else?

"What about Bernd Vollmer?" I asked. "He overheard us fighting that evening out on the patio, and he drove off shortly afterward, do you remember? I think he went to get Mirko from the forest. Maybe he found the diary at the same time?"

Julian was thinking this over.

"I don't know, Eva. What reason would he have?"

"Because we didn't help his son."

"Hmm, okay, but I can't imagine him taking the time to read your diary and then staging such an outlandish production. That's not really like him."

We stopped. True, I couldn't dismiss Julian's arguments lightly. Also, Bernd left this morning together with Mirko. Which didn't mean anything because the jeep was there when we got back a little while ago. But under the circumstances, Vollmer would have had enough time if he, say, dropped Mirko off somewhere—Mirko probably didn't have his own car—and then went to get a few photocopies done.

"Maybe it's some crazy person who enjoys snooping around in other people's lives. Maybe he found your diary by accident, read that you were staying at the mill—did you write that down in the diary?"

I nodded.

"And now he wants to mess with you." Julian got up and walked to the window. "You see it in the movies all the time. Mentally ill serial killer. He's probably sitting somewhere up in a tree, dressed in a raincoat, with a pair of binoculars, giving himself a hand job."

"Spare me the drivel, please!"

"You never know," Julian said gravely. "I really don't get this. Vollmer has much better ways of hurting us if he really wanted to. He could give my parents notice on the apartment, which wouldn't be a big problem seeing the kind of lease we have. Sneaky, well, I wouldn't put anything past him, but unfortunately, he has no reason to mess with you. Okay, so you didn't help him—but you offered help, and he refused."

"Can't you call Mirko by his real name for once?"

"What for? Hmm, now that I think about it—Sneaky doesn't even need a good reason. Whatever is going on inside that head of his, it's way beyond understanding anyway. But what speaks *against* him is that he just got a good beating—he knows exactly what will happen if he were to mess with us again. Sneaky is the biggest coward and full of self-pity; I can't imagine him risking getting beaten up just like that. Weird! So, either we're really dealing with a lunatic here, or we have overlooked something crucial." Julian turned toward me, asked, "Is there anyone else who might have a reason for you to leave, except maybe my friends? What did you do, what did you say, what did you see or hear that someone wants to get rid of you?"

"I don't know." After a pause, I added quietly, "But I've been going back and forth the entire time about whether or not I should go home to my parents. Sometimes I feel like you don't want me to be here either."

"Oh, nonsense!" Julian called out and threw himself onto the bed beside me, immediately making me feel queasy. "But that's not true! I love you, Eva!" He took me in his arms and hugged me very tight, and then we both cried a little. "You have no idea how sorry I am that we haven't had more alone-time together."

Boy, and he had no idea how sorry *I* was! I was in love with this boy up until a few hours ago! In love with his cute face, with his big round eyes, his mischievousness that was so often followed by shyness, his zest for life, and his tenderness. For me, he was the one I wanted to try out and experience love with—and what happened? A once-off at a point in time when we were both no longer unscathed, a first time that had been nice—but a first, anxiety-laden, painful, awkward first time, nonetheless. Now this vacation was unstoppably headed for an abyss, like a car on a roller-coaster ride: physical assault, extortion, a fatal accident, maybe even murder—everything imaginable had already happened, and it would probably just keep going along those lines. And what's waiting for us at the end? A separation?

A wave of nostalgia washed all over me. This boy, Julian, still belonged to me—because I did not leave, because we were both stuck here, both in shock and in mourning over Alina's death, and because I was now being blackmailed by a dangerous stranger. The dark, gloomy atmosphere that had cast a veil over the mill was holding us together.

Julian kissed me, on my neck, fiercely, or so it seemed—or was it me who kissed him first, intensely, urgently, as if my survival depended on it? I pulled my sweater over my head and grabbed his T-shirt. My first time, my last time, I thought. Am I even allowed to, now that Alina is dead? I'm like Alina, and I want to live. I kicked off my jeans. It seems so unfair if we don't really have each other, if nothing but bad things keep happening, and if I go home tomorrow and, ultimately, if my first love has been nothing but a few enjoyable hours and one major disaster. I want to feel alive; I don't want to be that girl who writes such terrible, stupid things in her journal and who has to feel ashamed about them; I want to leave all of that behind. I want to feel as proud, strong, liberated as I felt yesterday.

Julian seemed confused—after all, I was still crying—but then he saw that I really wanted what he thought that I wanted. Yes, I really wanted it. As inappropriate as it might be, to me it was all-important. I had this crazy, unrestrained feeling inside of me. I dug my fingers deep into his back. I wrapped my legs around him. I was loud, full of lust and full of sorrow all at the same time, and the most important thing to my survival was this: At this moment, where all that was left of me was flesh and body, I knew that I would be able to stand my ground, that I would be able to face the crucible that was Munkelbach.

"Wow, sometimes you're truly unbelievable," Julian whispered, his face red and his hair soaking wet. "That was amazing. I wouldn't have had the guts if you hadn't started."

I had to laugh and then suddenly cry again, but it was so exhausting and I was having such convulsions that it was enough to make me feel sick and for Julian to worriedly wipe the tears off my face.

"Evie? Did I do something wrong? Did I hurt you?"

"No, Julian, it's about Alina, and the guy blackmailing us, just everything…I don't know, it's all a bit much for me."

Julian rubbed his face.

"Yeah, that's true, it really is." He held me a little while longer, comforting me, and then he got up and got dressed. "Should I call the others? Maybe they've got some news."

"Yeah, please do. I have to find out who's trying to blackmail me."

He nodded and climbed down the stairs.

What choice did I have but to take a look at the threat letter one more time? It didn't matter how much effort that would cost me; if I wanted to defend myself, I had better find out what this person wanted from me first.

And so I reached for the letter and read it again—the words written in the letter, at least. I couldn't bring myself to look at my own text, was afraid that the words I had poured so much heart and soul into several months ago would turn against me, like my own body affected by some autoimmune disorder.

If you looked closely, my "blackmailer" did not reveal why he wanted to put pressure on me. He wasn't asking for anything, didn't even explicitly state that I should leave. But how else should I take his words, *Will you be staying long?* in this context, if not as a request to leave? Although some doubts remained, just like Julian I couldn't make heads or tails of it, except that he wanted to be rid of me.

But, unlike him, I did have a vague idea of what might be behind all of this: the fact that I thought to have recognized Bernd Vollmer and Alina in the background of Mirko's pictures, and that father and son both knew of this observation.

What if—and I felt queasy at the thought of it—what if both cases, Alina's death and this threat letter, were somehow connected?

Take it easy, Eva, I told myself; your imagination is running wild.

There must have been well over one hundred people at the party, and nobody would want to deny that Vollmer was one of them. He had to be there, if only for professional reasons. So it was perfectly normal for him to ask a female student if she was enjoying the cake from the buffet table, or if she and her classmates had been rehearsing any more amazing dance routines for their local dance troupe. However, in the photo they were obviously having a very intense conversation. That wasn't just innocent chitchat by any stretch of the imagination. Besides, hadn't Mirko said that his dad had the cell phone, back in the forest?

I reached for my new journal and opened up the one page that was full of notes. *Thursday night: Mirko is beaten up, tells me he doesn't have his cell phone on him (?), tells me he lost it, tells me—his dad had the cell phone!* I added. That's how it was, wasn't it? I decided to trust my memories a little more.

And right underneath those lines, I wrote: *On Saturday morning and in the presence of his dad, Mirko claims he doesn't have any files on his computer and that he lost the cell phone!*

An innocent mistake, a misunderstanding? Or, perhaps, deliberate deception?

I felt my heart pounding faster. The wall I was leaning against felt more wobbly than ever, and in my imagination the old mattress had turned into a waterbed. But I needed to keep my mind clear at all costs! Don't rush into anything, and don't jump to any conclusions with regard to the threat letter! Even if my memory served me right and if Mirko was contradicting himself—wasn't that understandable to a certain degree? Both times, he had been under a great deal of stress. The first time around, he thought I was one of his attackers and had been scared out of his mind; the second time he only just learned of Alina's death while his dad was breathing down his neck! Who, by the way, had not been particularly friendly toward his son—why?

I needed to talk to Mirko one more time, but this time alone and without any outside pressure. Only then would I tell Julian about it. This was my business, and I also didn't want him to think of me as hysterical. By now, I had a good idea of what he thought of people with psychological issues. Let him think that "the fox guy" was code for my other, red-headed, super smart boyfriend.

As I got up, I really felt the need to call my parents, but then I asked myself what I would tell them. Yesterday I had simply told them a lie, but today I wouldn't be able to tell them another one. Except, I didn't want to tell them the truth either; this would only needlessly upset them and unnerve me even further.

How had Mirko put it? Shaky half-truths make up half of everything people say, love the other half, and real truths—death?

Was it possible that he and I had a few things in common?

22

I had to hold on to the staircase railing and looked down, where I saw smoke rising from the fireplace. I overheard Julian's voice: "Eva is pretty frazzled. Yeah, totally. Hey, will you stop it? Okay, you went to the vigil at the school this morning. I believe you and I don't need to see any proof! I also can't imagine that Dustin or Chris… No, Laura, that's not what I meant. Anyways, I'd really appreciate it if you could come over. See you in a bit."

Julian turned off his cell phone and looked up at me.

"They're coming over. No news on Alina, except that they held some kind of a memorial service today at the school, and that there are tons of rumors."

I nodded wearily. Why should I be getting upset about seeing Julian's circle of friends again—the ones who had attacked me so viciously only yesterday? My time here with Julian had stopped being uninterrupted quality time a long time ago. Besides, Laura and friends weren't really on my list of suspects. Finding Alina, plus the thirty minutes or so we had waited in the forest, alone and terrified, and then all that questioning by the police—this super-intense experience seemed to have neutralized our mutual feelings of hostility. The only person who hadn't shared in this experience was Chris, and I was sure that I would find out whether or not he had written that nasty letter by just talking to him for a little while.

"Come sit with me, Evie. I'm cold."

"Okay," I said. Julian really looked very pale and almost a little sick. I took his outstretched hand; it was cold and clammy.

"You have to start wearing winter clothes, Jules, summer's over."

"Oh, *Jules* sounds nice. I like you saying it." He leaned against me.

"Okay." I rubbed my nose against his.

"I didn't even ask if it's alright with you that my friends are coming over. That was not okay, but please try to understand. I don't want to be alone here today. I have never felt unsafe here in the mill, never thought it scary to be out alone in the woods and cut off from the rest of the world. But now…"

He stopped, looked out the window. It was raining again. The wind must have picked up, too, because the pretty auburn leaves on the grape vine outside were floating, one by one, down onto the patio floor.

"Now all I want to do is pack you onto my bike—and off we go up to the highway, and then home."

I didn't say a thing. I was feeling the same way, of course. On the other hand, wasn't that exactly what the finder of my journal would want me to do?

My journal… My stomach churned at the thought of it. I imagined some big, fat, ugly guy with greasy fingers violently turning page after page, greedily hoping for something juicy, desecrating my innocent notes with his drool, tearing the binding off the slim, delicate book, and then, after having had his fun, carelessly tossing it aside.

"Eva? Don't cry! Do you want us to leave? Do you want me to go pack our bags and we'll go? Okay, we'll go! Let's forget about all of this; we can go on vacation some other time. We'll fly down south or something; we'll give *us* another chance!"

It was a tempting thought. Sun, warm weather, having fun. No forests, no friends, no nasty surprises.

"But that's exactly what he wants!" I jumped to my feet. "Oh man, Julian—I can easily tell you what I've written in my journal; it's nothing bad, nothing crazy. I could even tell Laura. The guy has nothing on me! It doesn't say that I'm secretly taking drugs or that I'm regularly stealing money from my parents. It's just a record of my pathetic little life, my everyday routine, my fears, my embarrassing moments. It's as if somebody stole all of your clothes in the mall, and you're standing there in your underwear!" My voice was getting loud, my face was red. I saw a warts-and-all mirror image of myself: the white lace on my underwear gray from too many washes, my belly, a little more potbelly than absolutely necessary, and the little stubbles on my legs growing relentlessly since I last shaved. I sure wasn't a monster, but I was no model, either. I was me, average and natural looking, and I had a right to my own privacy—it was nobody else's business!

"Eva, it's okay. I..." Julian got up, took my hand, didn't know what to say, waited.

This would have been a good moment to open up and talk honestly. I felt a great sense of openness in me and in him. We were getting close to one another again, even though I had slept with him fully expecting that we would split up. Now this beautiful feeling of love, of being in love could flare up again at any moment—yet right at that point a car drove up, and Laura, Mickey, and Dustin got out.

But maybe this early visit saved me from giving away too much of myself? If only you could know ahead of time!

Julian seemed to have noticed that we had just missed an important moment for regaining trust again in our relationship. We exchanged glances full of wistful sadness; it was as if both of us silently regretted this missed opportunity.

But I soon realized that I enjoyed having people around. Even though Chris of all people was missing because he had a handball match, it was okay for all of us to sit down by the coffee table, stare into the fire, and sample the first glass of hot mulled wine of the season.

It was with great sadness and pride that Laura showed us a birthday card Alina had hand-painted for her—Laura had been keeping the card in her wallet. She told us how people had bombarded her and Mickey with questions during the memorial service in the morning, and what kind of hogwash people in town were already talking about.

"So Cindy told me how she heard that Alina was found naked and died of eighteen stab wounds."

"Yeah, I heard that story, too," Dustin nodded. "Today I stayed in bed, I just had to. Then my mom brings me coffee at around noon and tells me that another girl has disappeared in Lower Lückendorf."

"A serial killer?" Julian asked, alarmed.

"Nah." Mickey made a dismissive gesture. "She's back. She slept at her boyfriend's house and forgot to tell her folks."

"But isn't it amazing how quickly such news makes the rounds?" Laura asked and nudged me in the side. It was supposed to be a friendly gesture, I guess, and I did give her a nod, but at the same time, I was also thinking at what incredible speed word-of-mouth news could travel if the finder of my journal were to follow through with his threats and post my innermost thoughts all over Munkelbach. Laura must have been having similar thoughts.

"So you're being blackmailed?" she asked and shook back her mane of ash-blonde hair. "Well, let me tell you, it wasn't us! Dustin was in bed all day, and Mickey and I spent the entire morning at school; you can ask anyone you want."

"You're not under any suspicion," Julian said quickly.

"Then who is?" Dustin snapped. "Chris?"

"No, no! We don't know! We can't imagine why anyone would want Eva to leave."

"That's not exactly what he's asking," I interjected.

Julian nodded.

"Right, I've been thinking about that, too. He's writing all this vague but very mean stuff. If you ask me, he's not interested in anything specific; he just enjoys messing with people."

"A guy like Sneaky," Laura suggested.

"Exactly."

Sheesh, they couldn't think of anything or anyone else, could they!

"Dude, this totally sounds like Sneaky." Mickey clenched his fists. "He's really asking to have his face smashed in again. Can I see that threat letter again? I know Sneaky's handwriting, and I would recognize it."

That was the last thing I needed: the gang beating up Mirko a second time around, on my account, and all because of some vague suspicion!

"That's not what I want, Mickey," I said sharply. "This guy copied parts of my journal, and my journal is nobody's business."

"Ooh, Eva's little secret," Mickey said, rolling his eyes dramatically and smirking at Laura in such a suggestive way that she started to giggle. The repulsion I had felt for them erupted again with full force.

"Yes, my secret!" I yelled, got up, and escaped out onto the patio. Even if they were right regarding Mirko: This was my business, and I wanted to handle it my own way.

The vine leaves swam in deep, dark rain puddles. I tilted my head back and looked up into the sky with great sadness. Suddenly and without my asking for it, passages of my journal started floating up into my consciousness; sentences I had jotted down in a great hurry and must have re-read a dozen times afterward (accompanied by deep sighs); words that had brought clarity and given me comfort, words that would seem trivial and idiotic to some but were extremely important to me as a way to reflect:

The fox guy has this really reassuring voice. I didn't like it at first. He never swallows his syllables, and he always pronounces Eva with a long "E." But for a therapy session, that kind of voice is not so bad. You feel like you're being carried on an idly flowing river, you forget how nervous you are and that someone is incessantly staring at you with these really intense eyes (we are sitting opposite each other and maintain, unless I'm nervously studying the patterns on the carpet again, eye contact), and that's what gets you talking pretty quickly.

I clearly remembered that this was how I had started my first journal entry. I had written it in tiny, terrified letters at the very top of the page, so close to the margin, in fact, that later I had to downright squeeze the date in above my writing.

He almost always stays calm. If you look at him, he will never ever avoid eye contact but instead stare back at you. As a matter of fact, he seems to almost always be looking at me—sometimes he looks puzzled, sometimes doubtful, but only ever friendly so far. The best thing I ever did was tell him that I was afraid he would reject me just like everybody else had. I'm glad I told him.

I had also been glad while I was writing it down. Now I felt like breaking my own fingers just to be able to un-write this text.

The fox guy always has this way of catching you by surprise. First, he will make some very blunt, very bold statement, then you protest, and now that he has you out of your box he can draw out the biggest, darkest secret from behind while he's busy reassuring you from out front. And you're sitting there, stiff with fear, while he's drawing you in with his soft, soothing voice, and you're staring at the box of tissues, and you're thinking: No, I'm not going to cry; the tissues are there so that I will cry, but I won't! And then you're back to the eye contact and he tells you something trivial, something memorized by heart, something kind, and then he gives you this professional, benevolent smile with well-practiced affection, and you nod obediently—sorry, deary, but you're the patient here—and then you take the bait: Yes, okay, so maybe I'm a little anxious; yes, I do have issues; yes, maybe you're right; yes, I really do need HELP.

I saw my own handwriting, little waves of turquoise-colored ink:

On the other hand, I don't need to be ashamed anymore to cry in front of the fox guy. First of all, he's used to it anyway, and secondly, no need to be ashamed to cry in front of someone you trust.

There was nobody here I was able to say that of, not even a little bit.

I would have loved to call the fox guy, right here and now. "Help me, please," I would have said. "I'm stuck in some kind of nightmare and I don't know what to do!" But I couldn't. It was Saturday, a little after six o'clock in the evening. Nobody worked at this hour.

And when I pulled my cell phone from my pocket to try to find comfort in my parents' voices, all I got was their answering machine.

23

If only Chris were here this afternoon! Even though he couldn't be dismissed as a potential letter writer, I would have loved to see him. A lot more than Mickey, at any rate, who was motioning for me to come back in while Julian was playing something for Laura and Dustin on his saxophone. I was still outside on the patio. I turned my back to the vacation home in disappointment, took a few steps toward the garden—and saw Mirko. He was sitting in the open patio door and was petting his cat.

"You better come back in, Midnight," he said without taking his eyes off me. "The weather is pretty lousy out here. Come on!"

Midnight didn't feel like it. She rubbed her head against his hand, stretched, and turned so that he would pet her where she liked it most. But she stayed outside.

Even though I had hoped for such an opportunity, this time I couldn't start our conversation with a lot of self-confidence. Instead, I just stood there timidly and was nervously thinking of something to say.

"Do you like cats?" Mirko asked—a question so unexpectedly simple and trivial that I hesitated even more. He didn't look mean or nasty at all, he seemed rather shy, and Midnight obviously adored him.

"Hmm." I would have loved to have a cat myself, but my mom was allergic to their hair.

"She's got another tick; you have to be careful out here in the woods."

"I think you have to be careful in general."

Mirko shrugged his shoulders.

"Yeaaah," he said slowly.

You could hear loud laughter coming from the apartment.

"Is the whole gang all gathered?"

I nodded.

"So? Are they drunk yet?"

I had to smile despite myself.

"How can you even stand being around them? If I were you…"

I would go home, I added in my mind. That was something I had wanted to do since my first evening, and yet I was still here.

"Well, it's none of my business." Mirko got up, reached for his cat, and wanted to go back inside with her. But Midnight had a mind of her own. She lashed out at him with her paw and jumped from his arms.

I grinned.

"Typical! Cats don't like it when you try to make them do something."

Mirko made a sorry face. "And her especially!" he said in a conversational tone. "How many times did my dad tell her not to sleep on his bed, but she doesn't care—especially not if it's freshly made."

"It's so nice to have a pet. But we live in the city, and... well."

Our conversation dried up. We stopped talking.

"Do you still want to know who Emra was with in the pictures?" Mirko asked after a while.

"I think I already know," I answered bitterly.

Mirko nodded.

"Please don't think I took the pictures because of Julian. I took thousands of pictures that night. I also didn't know that Julian had a girlfriend."

"Okay." So there it was: the clarity I wanted. Come to think of it, I already knew since this morning, because—in retrospect—Mirko's silence and Chris's hints had been clear enough. Only I didn't want to admit that Julian had betrayed me and, most importantly, didn't want to discuss it openly. Because I had been so afraid of my own anger, I tried to convince myself that I wasn't even sure if my anger was all that justified. That was a realization that could have come right from the fox guy.

"You know...I don't even know your name!"

"Eva."

"Eva, I don't know if you're even interested, but I'm not this mean and nasty guy everyone is always making me out to be. You don't have to believe me, but it's true." He lifted a hand. "Bye!"

"I believe you," I said quickly. And I really did. His version of the photo-blackmail story was no less plausible than Emra's. Maybe he had provoked it first, but Emra and Julian had both overreacted.

Suddenly I didn't want Mirko to leave. I felt connected to him. He rejected this group of friends as much as I did, was as excluded as I was.

He gave a thin smile.

"That's nice of you, but who cares." Then he decided to make an effort and added amicably, "How long are you staying?"

"Until tomorrow evening, but I don't really want to anymore. In a minute I'll be going to the super-awesome Tropic…" I mimicked Laura's voice and rolled my eyes.

Mirko gave a forced smile.

"Horrible place. Be careful not to lose Julian in all the excitement."

That was my cue. Something warned me deep inside, but I desperately wanted those photos. It would be easier to show my anger and to break it off if only I could show Julian the pictures to prove it. I told Mirko that I believed everything he said with regard to Emra, just not that he had lost his cell phone and that he hadn't saved the pictures to his PC.

"As stupid as it may sound, this cell phone is important. In the forest, you told me that your dad had it. Please! I need to have it!"

Mirko's face turned to ice, all his kindness disappeared.

"For the last time: I only looked at the pictures when I was in school, then I deleted the files on the school computer, then I lost the cell phone. Have you never lost anything?"

"I have, but I just don't believe you! Mirko, I really mean you no harm, I swear…"

"Oh, I see, so *that's* what you don't believe? You pick and choose what you believe, is that it? So whenever it suits you just fine you're being all nice and all and even talk to me, right? And why? I'll tell you why, because you need *me* to get your revenge!"

My face started burning. With shame and embarrassment, because I really was taking advantage of him; with anger, because I had made such a mess of it all, but also because I was allowing him to come down on me like that.

"It's not just about my own revenge, as you prefer to call it!" I shouted and realized that Dustin was opening the door at the same time. Maybe he was the reason why I had added that last part. I didn't want to seem like a fool in front of the gang; I wanted to show them that I wasn't stupid but that I noticed things that they themselves would never have noticed.

"It's also about Alina! She's in the pictures. I saw them, and who knows if whatever is in the pictures isn't important? Maybe it'll give the police a clue! You should maybe also think about that!"

Mirko didn't notice Dustin. He called me a "hypocrite" who had "no courage whatsoever" and was "blinded by jealousy," and then he slammed the door shut.

"Eva," Dustin said and lit a cigarette, "don't get so worked up! I have no idea why, but Julian really likes you. I wouldn't concern myself with Sneaky just because of a little bit of making-out. He'll only stick to you even more."

"Okay, Dustin, and you can stick your opinion up your ass!"

I was startled. I had never said anything like that to anyone! How would he react? Was I crazy?

He was cool and composed, just pulled up the corners of his mouth. Mickey would have totally freaked out; Dustin didn't really care much.

"So Alina was really in the pictures?" he asked and gave me a nod to come back into the house.

Inside, it was way too warm and filled with smoke. Julian was lying crossways in an armchair. He stretched an arm out toward me and held a mug of mulled wine out to me with his other hand. "Do you want some, Evie?" he purred. "Oh, I forgot: I'm not allowed to say *Evie* anymore!"

"Huh? Why the heck not?"

"It's against equal rights or something," Julian announced.

"Dude, come on!" Mickey shook his head, poked around in the fire.

I already had another sarcastic remark sitting on the tip of my tongue. I would have loved to tell them what I really thought of them: nothing on their minds but hanging out, boozing, and picking on other people. I wanted nothing more than to throw them out of the house, but I tried to restrain myself. I had made the decision to stay, and—given the circumstances—I wanted to avoid being alone as much as Julian did. And who knows, maybe I really was perfect for him; maybe I really was a hypocrite, as Mirko had called me.

"So what about Alina?" Dustin repeated with a serious face. "Does Sneaky have anything to do with it?"

"What?" Julian asked and shifted back into a sitting position. Laura took her eyes from her manicured fingernails, and I saw that she had been crying. Mickey stopped playing with the fire and pushed his hair back from his forehead. Dustin shoved me toward the couch and closed the patio door.

"Better we sort this thing out just between us."

I didn't feel like sorting anything out "just between us."

"I don't know, I'm not sure," I said evasively, feeling awkward and shifting under their attentive gaze. "All I can tell you is that Alina is in Mirko's photos, too. While he was taking pictures of Emra, she was talking to his dad."

"To Vollmer? How can anyone want to talk to him? He gave me an F in math, and before him I always used to get—"

"Mickey, nobody cares about that! Keep going, Eva. So, they were talking and…?"

"But I have no idea what they were talking about!" I snapped at Laura. I didn't appreciate her way of moving in closer one bit—as if she and I were best friends. Maybe we had been through something awful and terrible together, but that didn't make us friends. "I only saw that she was in the pictures. She was standing with Vollmer behind"—I hesitated for a moment—"behind you, Julian."

Julian didn't say anything. Nobody else did either. What's the point of denying something that's so obvious and that anyone at the party could confirm, not just Mirko. Julian had been making out with Emra. While I was counting down the hours in happy anticipation, while I believed that he was making preparations for the two of us, fixing the roof—hah, how could I have been so naïve—he and Emra had maybe even…slept together? I didn't really believe this, but didn't my feelings betray me often enough?

Now Julian narrowed his eyes, opened his mouth, got up, and I knew: in a moment, he would come over and try to explain. I jumped to my feet.

"Good thing that that's finally cleared up."

Glances were exchanged, and then Mickey said slowly, "Oh, okay, so they were there and were talking. We already knew that. Alina got on well with all the teachers, especially with Vollmer. He teaches art, and that's what she wanted to study in college."

"That was probably the last picture ever taken of Alina," Laura called out and covered her mouth with her hand in a dramatic gesture.

If anyone here was a hypocrite, it was definitely her!

"That was all you could see?" Dustin demanded.

"Yeah, that was it." That's all I would say, anyway. Because I really, really needed to get out of here, needed to be by myself. I wriggled my way free through Laura's legs, the coffee table, and the armchair—leaving Julian just standing there in a stunned stupor.

"Eva!" he said.

"We can't really use that," Dustin interrupted him. "Just because it might be the last photo ever taken of Alina, we shouldn't be getting Emra in trouble."

"That's right, dude." Mickey turned back to the fireplace.

I had so many questions on the tip of my tongue: Why hadn't Mirko gone to the police with the photos? Had he not noticed Alina in the background, just like Julian's friends? And what about his dad? Had he not noticed her either? Or had Mirko maybe not shown the pictures to his dad? But why then had he told me in the forest that Vollmer had the cell phone? Were they all just looking the other way, did they not care at all about what had happened to Alina? Or did someone else have something to hide—in addition to Julian and Emra?

24

Hoping for some quiet thinking time, I ran myself a hot bath. Afterward, I wrapped myself—smelling nicely of lotion—in someone else's fluffy bathrobe, sat down on the side of the bathtub, and forced myself to read the threat letter one more time and, most importantly, in full. In my journal, I had talked about my *worst secret*. Naturally, I didn't want anyone to find out about this at all—and the sender was obviously aware of this and had therefore removed the all-important passages of text. For now. This seemed to indicate that he wanted to use my past to blackmail me and drive me away.

Everyone in the group of friends had a motive. Dustin's alibi was weak, and Chris was still high up on the list. Even Bernd Vollmer might have a reason. And even Emra might want to be rid of me if she was serious about Julian. On the other hand, Emra could only have gotten hold of my journal indirectly and by mere chance.

Mirko didn't need a reason to harm others as far as the gang was concerned—but did I really want to trust them and their judgment? Mirko had been nice to me during our second conversation. He only closed himself off when I had asked for his cell phone.

Which brought me back to that last photo of Alina and Bernd Vollmer. Did that have something to do with it?

Should I maybe call the police and tell them everything? But I would then have to mention the blackmailing story, too.

How would the officers take this sketchy account of events?

There was something else that had me stuck: Why had the writer of the letter copied the part where I sing the praises of the fox guy, and planted it below the main section? That wasn't an essential part, and in my journal it was even in a different place altogether. Was it possible that the author wanted to achieve something other than just pure intimidation? The last sentence read: *Sometimes I need my fox guy as much as I need my Julian.*

A terrible, awful thought occurred to me: Julian! Did he have an issue with my not fully trusting him? Was it possible, just possible, that he had found my journal—maybe when we were out in the forest, or while I was in the shower, or after he had sent me upstairs to dry my hair? Could he have read it without being noticed, for example yesterday morning while I was sleeping? Before we drove to the mall, he had—while I was waiting in the garage—gone back to the apartment to get his wallet, which he allegedly left on the coffee table. But when exactly could he have made copies? When we were in the mall? Had we split up for a little while? And why was he being so passive when it came to finding out who had written the letter?

As I was going back and forth over this, I combed my hair from right to left and from left to right again, all the while ignoring the gentle vertigo caused by all these convoluted thoughts and by the awkward way I was holding my head.

All of a sudden, the entire gang started banging against the bathroom door from the outside. I started and was jolted out of my reverie; my vertigo increased, my knees turned into jiggly Jell-O.

"What the heck are you doing in there? Do you have low blood pressure again?" Julian's voice was meant to sound concerned, but when I opened the door, all I saw in his face was exasperation and suspicion.

"Eva, come on already! We want to go get something to eat before we go to the Tropic!" Mickey complained.

But Laura outstripped them all, as usual: "Wow, and here was me thinking: You know what, Eva is probably in the bathtub and cut her wrists!"

I would have loved to retort with something liberating, ironic, quick-witted, but I couldn't seem to manage right there on the spot. That picture of me Laura had conjured up—it paralyzed me. I said quickly, "I'll get dressed right away," and scurried into the bedroom.

"If you don't want to come with us, just stay here!" Mickey called after me, but I could hear Julian say, "No, she's coming with us. I don't want her all alone in here. It's too dangerous."

What did he mean by dangerous? Because the person who wrote that threat letter might turn up and attack me? Because Alina's killer was still out there? Or because he thought that I was a danger to myself?

Don't exaggerate, Eva, I told myself sternly as I was buttoning up my jeans. Laura talks nonsense all day long, and only someone who has read your journal would know that you're emotionally unstable. If you can pull yourself together—for just one more night—nobody will ever know. Don't give up! After all, you "went forth to learn fear," like the boy in one of Grimm's fairy tales. And yes, you will succeed!

25

We didn't talk much as we first drove to a shabby-looking fast-food stand and then to the Tropic, which was located in a small industrial park a few miles out of town. It wasn't even ten o'clock yet, but business had already started. At the club entrance, we met up with Emra, who was immediately informed by Laura that I was now in the know about her and Julian.

"I'm sorry," she said and came over to me. "Seriously, I regret that it happened. Julian and I, we like each other, sure, but that's it. I knew he had a girlfriend back home, and he knows that he's totally out of the question for me. We were fooling around, drank too much that night. What happened just"—she snapped her fingers searching for the right words—"just came over us like that. I'm really sorry, Eva. I made a mistake."

Made a mistake…that was the exact wording Julian had used before. When was that again? I couldn't remember anymore, didn't want to know how many obvious signs I had missed.

"Really, it was just innocent fun. In the pictures, it looks a lot crazier than it actually was. There was nothing more to it than some snuggling and a peck on the cheek. It woul never have come to anything else because we were surrounded by thousands of people."

"Whatever, Emra." I didn't feel like listening to her excuses and pointedly sat down on one of the platforms at the edge of the dance floor, while the others continued on toward the cocktail bar.

"Nobody would even have remembered it or gotten so worked up over it if it hadn't been for Mirko's pictures." Emra was persistent and sat down beside me.

"Your problem, not mine." I scanned the youths moving in front of me on the dance floor. Most of them were younger than we were. They probably came here because there was nothing else to do in the area, and because the drinks were cheap. Wait a minute! Wasn't that Chris over there, trying to make his way through the crowd? Should I go to him, speak to him? But what if he is the guilty one?

Emra tugged on my sleeve.

"When Mirko gave me the pictures on Thursday morning, I locked myself in the bathroom and cried."

So was I supposed to feel sorry for her now, or what?

Chris disappeared from my field of view. Finally I said, more to myself, "I know the feeling when you're being blackmailed and intimidated. It pulls the ground right from under your feet."

"Yeah. Have you had it happen to..." Emra sounded genuinely surprised—deeply concerned and interested.

My gruff, armored exterior started showing cracks. I sighed. In all honesty, it had been stupid to suspect her. After all, she could only have gotten hold of the diary from one of the other friends and would have needed someone to drive her to the Rauschenmühle water mill. I pushed the whole Julian issue aside for now and at that point simply took her for a girl who had the same problems as me. In a couple of sentences, I told her about my diary.

Emra shook her head.

"I can't imagine why anyone would do such a thing. But there are such people. I mean, what was it that Julian and I did? We were just being silly. Seriously! The whole thing couldn't have lasted longer than five minutes. But Sneaky seems to think that he can drive the two of *you* apart and mess up *my* life. What a jerk! And then you have other people who are totally insensitive and don't even think twice about what kind of a chaos they're causing. Take our high school principal, for example: Two weeks after summer break, he introduced a new dress code at the school. He doesn't want girls to turn up in school as if they're going clubbing. He wants 'appropriate clothing.' And right after he said it, pictures of Alina started appearing on our website."

Suddenly, I was all ears.

"Pictures of *our* Alina?"

"Yeah. I didn't see the webpage because the school administration took the pictures down the very next day. But as far as I heard, the pictures must have been extremely unflattering. Like, how Alina's bending down and how her breasts are almost hanging out. Apparently, you could see all the way to her underwear, you know…"

"Miniskirt and maxi legs, that sounds like Laura!"

"Laura's way too chicken and too stupid to pull this off. Besides, she would never be able to get the password for the website. Students don't know the password. One of the *teachers* must have added the pictures to the official text of the school administration. That's why the principal made such a big show of apologizing to Alina and her family, and now the dress code is off the table. There was a lot of discussion about this. The whole thing was an honest mistake, or so they say, but I don't believe that anymore." Emra smoothed back her jet-black hair, made a grim face, and lowered her voice. "You see, Alina had her suspicions. She came to see us only a few days ago because she was tutoring my little brother in English. She said that it was no accident that it was her in the pictures, of all people. Somebody wanted to intimidate her and mess with her, that's what she claimed. I always thought that was nonsense, especially because Alina has always had a vivid imagination. But now she's dead."

I felt my hair stand on end. Intimidate, mess with, expose—just like that, on a whim. Didn't that sound exactly like what was happening with my journal and me? What if it was the same perpetrator? Hadn't I been searching for some kind of a connection all along?

And hadn't Julian said that we were similar, Alina and I?

"D-did you tell the police about this?"

"No!" Emra gave an awkward laugh. "Do you have any idea what my dad would say if I got involved with the police?"

"But you should anyway!" And I should have, too—a long time ago.

"No!" She got up and wiped away our newly found friendliness and intimacy with a single, abrupt sweep of her hand. "I know nothing. What do *you* think? Alina didn't tell me who her suspect was. Hey, look, I'm really sorry about what happened, but I don't want any trouble!" She vanished into the crowd.

26

"Wait!" I yelled and tried in vain to follow her. There was no getting through this jungle of twitching arms, legs, and heads. I quickly lost sight of her.

Where were the others? What if I had lost them for good?

I stopped, suddenly alone in an environment that seemed very hostile to me. A dark-haired guy gave me a wink with overtly sexual undertones; a pimply blond guy tested his flirty eyes on me, too; a third guy ran into me as if by accident; and the two girls sitting at the neighboring table were definitely giggling and talking about me. "You're imagining things, Eva," I told myself in a stern voice, but I really wasn't convinced. That feeling of someone watching was so strong that my mind was unable to fight it. Fear wrapped itself around my legs, my chest, my throat. In a moment, I wouldn't be able to move. I had to do something, quick!

What would the fox guy recommend? Maybe walk over to the bar, order a mineral water, drink, calm down, try to connect all the little dots of information, find Julian, and then, last but not least, call the police?

I was just about to put my plan into action when I heard the DJ turning down the music and—like a ra host—devoting some time to customer requests. The audience must be pretty young or pretty stupid to appreciate this kind of thing.

"Before we move on to our next hit, chosen by Caroline for Dominic—*the message is in the song*—I will start by reading a few love letters, like we do every Saturday at eleven to eleven. The first note, just a second"—you could hear him tearing open an envelope—"is for *Eva in the mill*."

I turned to stone and desperately clung to one of the bar tables. I knew what would follow, and I was unable to stop it.

"Wow, somebody is positively gushing with all that L.O.V.E. You know the rules: no more than three sentences. But alright, let's read it, maybe we'll like it."

Did they know, did they sense…? Those girls over there, for example, who kept looking over, giggling, sticking their heads together—did they know that it was me the DJ was talking about?

Who else? It could only be me, of course. You could tell from a mile off. Well, was anyone *else* standing here in the middle of this big, stupid, monster disco looking as if she was about to have a heart attack?

The DJ cleared his throat.

"*That whole horrible story was not my fault. I was a suspect because nobody liked me, nobody knew me, and because nobody would believe me.* Aha! A confession! I think the next part will be, 'Please forgive me, Eva-in-the-mill!' Well, do we want to hear it?"

The DJ was an idiot, and the audience lusted for ▪mething juicy. "*Even my fox guy, who was after all my confi-▪t, my go-to person, had his doubts about my story.*"

I squealed. He didn't! I had only been afraid that he might! I had written those words against my own better judgment, out of self-pity, or maybe to hurt myself—I wasn't sure. All I knew was that he had believed in me from the very beginning.

The thought of this gave me strength. Not that I was able to use this strength in any sensible way, shape, or form. No, I just charged through the club like a madwoman. As I fought my way through the crowd toward the exit, bumping into people, knocking over glasses, punching and pushing, I heard the DJ say, "Well, friends, that was a very strange love letter. Let's play some music instead, what do you say?"

I made a run for the door, past the bouncers, and was outside. After I had taken ten, fifteen steps, I disappeared in between parked cars and squatted down, just sat down on the asphalt.

I could smell the deep-frying fat coming from the nearby fast-food stand. Pools of motor oil, cigarette butts, and spit stains caught my eye. But I had to stay here, had to stay sitting down. I was extremely nauseous. My knees were shaking. I remembered that horrible old story, and my memories of it pounded through my head at full speed, like a hurricane.

During the school trip, someone had cut holes in all the T-shirts, shirts, pants, and underpants of a certain girl. I didn't like that girl; she loved torturing me. I was alone in my room that night, reading and counting the minutes until the whole dumb school trip—that my parents had made me go on—would be over. But it wasn't me cutting holes in that girl's clothes. We never found out who it was, but it wasn't me. That girl and her friends' revenge had been to pick on and torture another girl the following night until she peed her pants in fear and, out of utter shame, almost jumped off the roof of the youth hostel that we were staying in. That girl, that soiled, weak, lowly girl: that was me.

I bit my knuckles. The fox guy didn't reject me then, so I shouldn't reject myself now.

And I didn't need to. Because it could no longer be denied: I was on somebody's hit list. Somebody was out to get me. Maybe in the same way that someone had been out to get Alina?

Fear paralyzed me, drained away my strength to think straight. Even Julian's outlandish speculation that a crazy person, an as-seen-on-TV serial killer, might be after me didn't seem so farfetched anymore in its brutality.

I knew that I really had to call the police. But first I had to find Julian and get him to take me to a safer place. Even though our bond of trust was broken, he was still the only person here I could and would turn to. I couldn't bring myself to go back into the Tropic, however, where everyone would be staring at me. It didn't matter that I kept telling myself in my sensible voice that nobody would make any connection between me and the letter the DJ had read out loud. Even the fact that most people probably hadn't listened anyway, that in all likelihood nobody was even interested in the whole thing, and that almost certainly not every single person had laughed at me—even that fact couldn't change my mind. I was paralyzed, was having a blackout episode, whatever you want to call it: I just could not go back into the Tropic. Impossible. I was torn between what I had to do and what I couldn't do, and this made me furious and even more panicky. How was it possible that I was my own worst enemy?

27

"Eva?" As faint and shy as that voice was, it startled me.

I jumped to my feet, ready to run.

"It's me, Mirko."

A relieved squeak escaped my lips. Mirko, I knew. To be the ugly duckling in front of him was bearable—after all, we were both part of the same species.

He gently touched my arm.

"I overheard the DJ reading that letter. I wasn't quite sure what to make of that so-called love letter, but when I saw you running for the door I knew right away that it must be something awful."

I was fighting back the tears.

"Somebody found my journal and is having a jolly good time going public with it."

Mirko was silent for a moment. Then, as if reading my thoughts, he said, "Come on, I'll get you out of here. Unless you want to go back in there?" Resolutely, he linked arms with me and pulled me with him toward the jeep, which was parked close by.

"But..." I said in baffled protest.

"Nothing but! Has Julian cooked this up?"

"Julian?" I stopped right beside Mirko's parked car.

"I've known him for a long time, and I know him well. First, you can't even begin to imagine what kinds of devious ideas he might think of sometimes. You're thinking: He's my friend, and he is, but he'd better not get the impression that you're less useful to him than he wants you to be. *Then* he will leave you hanging; *then* he will mess you up."

I couldn't reply, felt as if the parking lot I was standing on had a basement underneath it, and that the asphalt was swinging back and forth to the sound of the bass booming from the dance club.

Mirko opened the passenger door.

"I just saw him again with Emra, and so I thought you were having a fight."

"W-we are. But I didn't lose my diary in the house; I lost it in the forest that evening, when you were being..." I really only wanted to explain to Mirko that several people could have found my journal—Chris, for example, and he was in the club now, too!—but now I was back to the very beginning, to the moment when Mirko was being beaten up, and Mirko promptly said, "Oh, you mean the evening when the four of them were coming at me with everything they had? The evening when they beat the hell out of me and I almost ended up in the hospital? And all because I was taking party pictures for the school newspaper and foolishly also took some pictures of the 'secret' couple? How is it my fault when people get all testy just because you confront them with the truth?"

Mirko wanted to push me into the car without much further ado, but I struggled against him. Who said that I wanted to drive off into the sunset with him? I wanted to ꞁd Julian, wanted to call the police!

"Listen, please," he pleaded. He was all fired up. I could tell from his breathless voice and frantic moves. "I can prove that it's exactly as I told you. I didn't lose the cell phone, it's right here in the car. If you want, I'll show you the pictures. There's a whole series of them. In one of them, you can clearly see that Emra was well aware of my taking pictures of her and Julian. But she didn't do anything about it; she was so horny for your boyfriend that she just kept on making out with him."

"So you still have the cell phone? Why have you been lying to me this entire time?"

"Because..." Mirko lowered his head in embarrassment. "For one, because I was afraid your friends would attack me again."

"They are not my friends!"

"I know that now! I trust you, Eva, why else do you think I'm telling you all this? The other reason is a lot more important."

I gave him a blank stare.

"Just give me a little time, and I will tell you what it's all about."

"Why me?"

"Who else? Everybody here seems to be prejudiced against me! Even you seem to have reservations about getting into a car with me, as if I were a...a monster! What did the others tell you about me? That they call me Sneaky, for example? Do you know why? Why I used to walk around on tiptoes? Because I was scared of them! I thought that if I don't draw attention to myself, if I don't say anything, if I manage to be invisible, then maybe they will forget to take their frustrations out on me!"

Now it was my turn to touch Mirko's arm gently, in the same way he had done to me earlier.

"Thank you." Mirko nodded slowly. "There's a pretty good ice cream parlor in town that's still open. Can I buy you an ice cream?"

I hesitated. "Yeah."

Why did I postpone my own plans and actually got into the jeep with him? Why didn't I at least question what Mirko was doing in a nightclub that he himself had called a "horrible place" and that was only frequented by people who didn't like him?

Because I wasn't afraid of him. I thought that fear was something we had in common, something that we had formed—little by little—inside our own heads, something that was pure fiction and that was possible to overcome.

28

The car was very neat and tidy inside and had that new car smell. There was a travel bag sitting on the passenger seat that Mirko had to move to the backseat first. Then he took the ignition key, turned his head toward me, smiled at me—nicely, but also a little irritating. His eyes were wide open in the same way the fox guy's eyes sometimes are, and I saw such a profound, meaningful expression in them that I instinctively grabbed the car door handle and said, "I would like to see the pictures *before* you start the car."

"No problem. You don't trust me, Eva, but hey—I'm used to it." Mirko made a big show of reaching back toward the backseat, dug out the cell phone from the travel bag, turned it on, quickly flipped through the pictures that were saved on it and which I could only see as colorful blobs from where I was sitting. He then held the phone up to my face without it ever leaving his hands, but still close enough that I was able to see the photo he had pulled up. Emra was in the picture again, and—clearly visible this time—Julian. Thankfully, they weren't kissing and making out at that point but just stood very close together. Emra looked directly into the camera and stuck her tongue out at the photographer.

"You see? They knew exactly that I was taking pictures."

"Your dad and Alina aren't in it."

"They had already left at that point."

I stopped short.

"What do you mean they left?"

Mirko didn't say a word.

My heart was beating faster. Very slowly, I said, "You mean they left to get a beer or something?"

More silence. Mirko's eyes were so heavy with meaning right now that I already guessed what he was going to say. Though I still couldn't believe it.

"How do you mean, 'They had already left at that point'?"

Mirko took his time replying, played with the ignition key as if to raise my suspense.

Finally—I had already started shifting nervously in my seat—he asked, "Can I trust you, Eva?"

"Yes, of course." This was easily said if you're about to burst with excitement and curiosity.

"Alright. I'm not sure, you know. Maybe it's a mistake to count on you. Normally I don't trust anyone, and I get by just fine. But there has to be a first time for everything, right?"

I wanted to say, "Get to the point, Mirko!" But he was being so serious that I didn't dare to pressure him, and so I just nodded instead.

"I found this letter today." Mirko pulled an envelope from his jacket's inside pocket. "It's from Alina."

Even though I had expected it to be about Alina, the mention of her name electrified me. Her handwriting, which was familiar to me from Laura's birthday card, immediately caught my eye. *Bernd* was written on the envelope.

Butterflies and exotic birds fluttered, flapped their wings all around his name.

"I give it to you because I don't know who else to turn to. I would like nothing more than to just forget and burn it; I really just want to run away and be alone. But at the same time, I wish I could talk to someone. Do you know that feeling? That feeling when you're on the edge, in between longing and being afraid? For me, trusting someone feels like allowing someone else's hand to guide me over a tightrope." Mirko grinned to himself. "I'm afraid of heights, you know."

His chitter-chatter was annoying. I felt the urge just to tear the letter from his hands. But I could feel that I wouldn't be able to pry anything else out of Mirko if he got the impression that I was more interested in information regarding Alina than in his own little emotional state. So I said yes.

"You know that feeling, right?"

"Yes." Impatient. Even though it was true: for a long, long time I had wished for someone who would understand me, and still I had fought tooth and nail against going to therapy. And then I just got real lucky when I met the fox guy. I had liked him immediately. Maybe, or so I thought, Mirko also needed a fox guy.

"I don't know why, Eva, please don't get me wrong, it's not supposed to be a come-on or anything, but I wouldn't show this letter to anyone else except for you. Maybe I shouldn't say this, but I think you're different from everyone else. I feel so close to you, like we're soul mates."

That unexpected compliment felt good, even though I was bursting with curiosity and felt very, very impatient right now. Nevertheless, I stopped short. Mirko and I did know each other well enough for him to say this to me. On the other hand, hadn't I felt exactly the same way only a few hours ago?

At long last, he handed me the envelope. There was only one sentence written on the letter paper: *Will I see you later at our usual place?*

I whistled through my teeth. Well, well: Bernd and Alina! I had been wondering about their obvious intimacy in the pictures. Did they have an affair? Was this what Mirko had been hinting at when he talked about the "secret couple" earlier? What if Alina had spent her Tuesday night with Bernd Vollmer, out in the forest by the castle ruins?

"Do you know what this could mean?" I asked Mirko.

"Of course. They were secretly having an affair."

I tried to picture Bernd Vollmer in my mind: athletic, good-looking. And if you add a few shared interests or hobbies on top of it, he could probably be considered attractive. There was really nothing wrong with it. Except the fact that Alina was dead.

"What now?" I asked Mirko. "He's your dad."

Mirko gave a sob. "But that's exactly it! You have to help me!"

I was dumbfounded. Wasn't it *he* who had wanted to help *me*? Or were the two of us both in need of help? Were we relying on one another?

"If I can…," I whispered, struck by the possible consequences of such news. This made Bernd Vollmer one of the prime suspects in the Alina case. He was even a potential candidate when it came to my journal. Maybe he found it right next to his beaten-up son. What if he wanted to get rid me by taking my journal public so that I wouldn't cause too much of a stir, what with me talking about the school party pictures? Bernd Vollmer had probably also put pressure on Mirko so that his son would stick to his story of not having saved any pictures to the computer and of having lost the cell phone. I was surprised that he hadn't taken the cell phone away from his son sooner. Whatever the case may be, his son had now turned to me, had volunteered to pass on everything he knew.

I started getting the rare feeling of my ego being boosted. Mirko trusted me, and really only me. Because—contrary to everyone else—I had been open and straight with him; because he saw in me an honest, dependable, intelligent friend.

"Let's just talk, okay?" Mirko looked at me imploringly, clumsily wiping tears off his cheeks.

"Alright."

"Thank you, Eva, thank you." A moment later, he started the engine and stepped on the gas. He was obviously in a hurry to get as far away from the Tropic as possible, because he drove on to the main country road without ever slowing down or braking and without looking to the left or right.

"That thing between my dad and Alina was going on for weeks already. They would talk about art and exhibitions for hours, wanted to convert the mill into an art studio. I always said that he was acting childish, that it wouldn't end well, that Alina was only using him, and…"

I interrupted him: "Not so fast! I'm going to be sick. And you're not going to solve anything by speeding."

"But I'm not! I'm driving normal! But I'm nervous. Now you tell me what you're thinking about this whole thing. She was only using my dad for her high school diploma and her stupid art, and he…what do you think he wanted? They always went to the castle ruins to have sex! Can you imagine? They were worse than your beloved Julian with Emra. Come on, tell me what you're thinking! She's your age; she could be your sister." Mirko's wails were getting louder and more and more frenzied. "He wasn't thinking of me at all in all of this; a few times he even invited her over to the house—this big fat cow—our house, I even caught them in Mom's bed, and Alina wasn't embarrassed or ashamed, not even a little bit. She just laughed and said I was narrow-minded and way too conservative and said that I, yes *I*—"

"It's alright, Mirko. Please keep your eyes on the road."

I understood how extremely conflicted he must be. I felt sorry for him, but one thing was very clear to me: Even if he trusted me so much that he would call his dad a murderer in front of me, even then I had to make sure that I left this car in one piece as quickly as possible and that I got the two of us back to civilization, back to where there were more people. Mirko on his own was way too agitated, way too unpredictable.

29

I pulled my cell phone from my jeans pocket, while he barely managed to get out of the way of an oncoming car.

"Be careful!" I dialed Julian's number.

"I haven't had my driver's license for very long! I...Eva, don't!" Lightning-fast he leaned over to me and snatched the cell phone from my hands. He lost control of the car. The jeep started skidding across the road. I screamed, terrified by Mirko's behavior and by the trees that started appearing in front of the windshield.

"Soorrrrry!" Mirko tried to get the jeep back onto the road and into his lane. I was clinging to the grab handle. And now, of all moments, vertigo closed in on me! Oh, how I wished that for once my crazy, broken head wasn't getting in the way so that I might actually take my cell phone back from Mirko while he was busy steering the car. But my own body forced me into paralysis. I had to focus all of my energy on not losing my bearings entirely and throwing up. What a loser I was!

After about a minute, the jeep was steady again and moving along the road at normal speed.

"Well, I think that did the trick." Mirko sounded relieved suddenly all cool and collected, and no longer weepy at a

He slowed down as we approached an intersection, fully in accordance with traffic regulations. *Munkelbach, 1.9 miles* read the sign—but he turned the wrong way.

And now my panic was back.

My pounding heartbeat joined the furious spinning inside my head; I could feel it in my throat and on my tongue. My throat was so cramped up that every sound I made pricked like a needle.

"What are you doing? Are you trying to kidnap me?" I sounded pitiful. I *was* pitiful.

I have failed, Dr. Fuchs. I got into the car because I thought Mirko was harmless, because I was being bigheaded, because I wanted to stick it out at all costs, I have no idea why. But it's too late now; this is me paying the price for my own stupidity.

"Kidnap? What? Why? We're going to get ice cream. Everything in Munkelbach will be closed by now. We have to drive to the next big town."

"I never agreed to this!" You could hear the desperation in my voice, and I hated myself for it.

"But that's what I meant. Everybody knows that Munkelbach shuts down for the night at seven."

"Then give me back my cell phone! If I don't call Julian to tell him I'm okay, he will call the police."

That was a weak attempt at bluffing, and Mirko didn't fail to notice. He snorted with laughter.

"Do you really think he's going to miss you? Now that he's all alone with Emra? Oh, I see, you don't want him to worry," he purred, turned to face me, and pulled an ironically indulgent face. "You still love him."

Was it possible that Mirko was playing with my fear?

"Julian will miss me."

"Alright, alright," Mirko grumbled gruffly. "Calm down already! I was only kidding. Of course you can call him. I didn't want to scare you or upset you. I only took the cell phone from you because I needed to ask you this one thing: Don't tell him about Alina's letter, promise me! That's all, Eva. Hey! Did you really think I was going to kidnap you? Am I crazy? Why the heck would I do that?" He looked over to me, eyes wide open now, and I saw his tears shimmering again. "You're making stuff up in your head, Eva. You've got way too much imagination! Hey, listen, I like you. I mean it! I'm just totally bummed out about that story with Alina. Can't you understand?"

He baffled me. He seemed weak and dangerous all at the same time. I didn't know what to do, and so I gave him the reply he wanted to hear: "I won't tell Julian about the letter. But I will tell him where we're going."

"Great, thanks." Mirko slowed down a gear and turned into a side road. "Shortcut." Then he took my cell phone and tossed it to me. "If Julian wants to come join us, we'll be at the Casablanca. He should know where that is."

I was unbelievably happy to hold my cell phone in my hands again. While I awkwardly dialed Julian's number and in my panic of course pressed a wrong key, Mirko turned on the CD player.

"How do you like the sound?"

"Hmm, it's good," I said while I tried to dial again.

"I've got a selection of CDs in the glove compartment. Take a look and see if there's anything you like."

Was Mirko now giving me the good friend act? Or cou[ld] I really breathe a sigh of relief because I had, once ag[ain] gotten all worked up over nothing? Maybe he was as excessively awkward as I was excessively scared? But had I ever been scared for no reason during this vacation?

My phone was establishing the connection to Julian's number. I stared at the cell phone display, and the next moment I bit my lip in disappointment: no network.

"Not working?" Mirko asked with a sideways glance. "Try again in a minute when we're over that hilltop there. Reception can be very patchy here."

"Right." I pressed the redial button.

Mirko drove more slowly now, almost at a crawl.

"What I wanted to propose, as well: You can spend the night at my place. Not in the mill, but in a little heated hunting lodge that's part of our property. You'll be safe there and you'll get some peace and quiet, also from Julian. And in the morning you can just take your time and catch the train home."

Darn reception! What was Mirko talking about?

"That's very nice of you, but I think I'd rather not."

"I understand. I'm only offering you this because I'm so glad that you're not prejudiced against me and that you really are there for me. You're my go-to person, Eva."

"What?"

"Oh, nothing, I think I heard that somewhere."

That was impossible. "Go-to person" was exactly the name I had given the fox guy in my journal. I had invented it, it was my fantasy word.

Suddenly my fingers started shaking so much that my cell phone dropped into my lap.

Mirko didn't fail to notice. Quickly he said, "Ah, I ember where I heard the word before: in the club, you know, in the letter the DJ read out loud, this word was mentioned in it. I liked it."

I couldn't make a sound.

"Oh, that was totally insensitive of me again, right?" Mirko turned onto a dirt road, stopped the car, turned off the engine but left the ignition on—as if he wanted to start the engine again at any moment. Then he leaned over to me very quickly. "I'm sorry that I reminded you of that thing! Here's me wishing for someone so desperately, someone who'll look after me, and no sooner do I think that I've found that person that I'm already screwing things up!"

But that was exactly what *I* had wished for so desperately *from the fox guy*: that he'd look after me! He hadn't said anything then, just kind of hinted at something like a "yes"—something in between a "yes, I know" and a "yes, I will"—and then he had closed his eyes, smiling. I had taken up an entire page in my diary trying to figure out that fox-specific facial expression.

Mirko must have read it!

I dug my fingers into the cell phone.

Okay, so Bernd Vollmer, my prime suspect, had a deep, long scratch on his arm. And maybe also had a motive to kill Alina. After all, it was possible that she wanted to go public with their secret affair, or that he was jealous, or...

But that didn't seem to fit. Alina had been in love with Vollmer, had been making plans for their future together. And shortly before, they had shared an affectionate laugh. Besides, would someone like him ever go to a nightclub just to hand my diary over to a DJ? That seemed a lot more like his son to me.

My lower lip was bleeding.

"You're alright?"

Yesterday, Midnight, the cat, had instinctively jumped away and lashed out at him when he tried to grab her and take her back into the house. But I didn't have any claws. I didn't even have pepper spray on me.

"Yeah, I'm fine," I lied and was surprised at how naturally my mouth and tongue were moving. My body had switched to autopilot.

"About your diary...okay, please, so don't freak out: I know what's in it. I snuck into my dad's study today and did a little snooping around. That's when I found Alina's letter and also your diary. But I hardly read any of it, I swear."

Why the heck did I have to cry now of all times?!

Mirko grabbed my hand.

"I'm really sorry!"

I couldn't see a car jack or anything that I could have used to hit him over the head with.

"Eva, can you forgive me? I mean, I didn't really do anything! At first, I didn't really know what I had there in front of me. And I didn't want to read it, honestly, I just started, you know, and then...then I felt that..." he sniffled, rubbed his eyes, "...that you're very close to me. You're exactly like me, you see. Nobody else seems to really get you; you're like an outcast to everyone else. I cried and I cried, that's how much it moved me. I was feeling so sorry for you, and I really, really wanted to just give you a hug."

I remembered that passage from my journal that the DJ had read out loud in the dance club: *Nobody likes me, nobody knows me, nobody will believe me.* It almost felt as if Mirko had ‍aken the words right out of my mouth.

"Can I give you a hug, Eva? Please?"

I nodded stiffly, all the muscles in my body tensed up. Mirko cuddled up to me, didn't seem to notice that I was sitting there like a block of ice. Even though I couldn't prove a single lie he had told me, I slowly started trusting my inner voice again. I should have listened to it right from the beginning, and I shouldn't have allowed everyone else as well as my own lack of self-confidence to cause all these mixed feelings. All in the past now. From now on, *I* will look after *me*.

Looking over Mirko's shoulder, I tried to assess the situation. Yet again, I found myself in a deserted, wooded area, in the middle of the night, unable to count on outside help. Mirko had parked in an empty, desolate parking lot intended for hikers. Right in my field of vision, illuminated by spotlights, I saw the Munkelbach Spring—as if I had returned to the source of all evil. *No Drinking Water* read a wooden sign above the metal tap.

Should I try to escape? Into the unknown darkness in which Alina had died? With my vertigo and in these high heels? Would I even stand a chance? Was there no other option?

Being as calm and gentle as I could, I gently pushed Mirko away from me, wiped away my tears, and said, "It's okay. I believe you. But I must look like a mess. I can't go to the ice cream place looking like this. Do you have a tissue for me?"

"Of course." He turned toward the back, opened the travel bag that was still sitting on the backseat, all the while keeping his eyes on me.

Tear open the door and make a run for it? No way.

"Thanks. There's water over there. Would you m' soaking the tissue a little?"

"Sure."

Was he thinking about pulling the key from the ignition? What for? He knew that I was only sixteen and couldn't drive yet. Giving me a little pretend-friendly wave, Mirko walked backward toward the spring water tap. As soon as he got there, all I needed were two seconds to turn on the interior lights, and an additional seven to find the push button for the central locking system. When Mirko realized what was happening and made a dive for the car, you could hear a loud click: he was locked out; I was locked in.

30

"What do you think you're doing? Open up!"

Never in a million years. If I couldn't run, then I could at least escape his grasp: with him on the outside and me on the inside.

"I thought we were friends!" Mirko tried sweet-talking his way back in, pulled a sad face, pretended to be terribly cold. "That's not funny. It's really cold out here!" And begging, pleading: "Now open up, come on!"

I have always found it difficult to say no. Even now I was seriously reconsidering what I had done, and whether I was doing him wrong. What did I really know about him for sure, except that he had read my journal? Was I able to prove that he'd really only known its contents since this afternoon instead of from much earlier? I tried to recall our encounter from this morning; Mirko's fancy saying, "Shaky half-truths make up half of everything people say." At first, I thought he was talking about shaky half-truths in terms of a lie. But then he had immediately guessed that I might be shaky, as in dizzy. Coincidence? He was now pressing his face against the glass. "Eeeeva! I'm really sorry about that thing with your diary. But please don't think that I would even think of telling anyone. Oh man, I took the diary fro my dad, and in fact, I wanted to give it to you when we got to the ice cream place. You know, make a little ceremony of it! But if you open the door, you can have it back right away."

Don't let him trick you! Remember this morning? There was Bernd, excessively shocked by Alina's death, which by now of course I was able to put into perspective—now that I knew about their secret relationship. But Mirko... How had he reacted? I couldn't remember exactly: he had been sad, sure, but had he also been surprised?

Please stop thinking! Mirko was at the school party until the end, wasn't he?

"Eva, please, let me in! It's starting to rain. Just think of your diary!"

You'd better think of your survival!

"For the last time, Eva, open up the doors! This is my car. You have no right to lock me out!"

I leaned back into my seat. Okay, one thing at a time. Don't freak out. Think of the fox guy. First, calm down; next, act; find words, speak: "Go away, Mirko! I will only open the doors if you go get Julian."

"Are you crazy? How am I supposed to do that? My cell phone's not working either!"

"Then walk."

"What did you say?" He hammered his fists against the car window. "What do you want from me, Eva? Do you think you can mess with me?!"

"I want you to call Julian. Get him to come here and pick me up."

Was that a good plan? I hoped it was!

Mirko reached into the inside of his jacket, froze. A moment later I realized what was going on. His cell phone was still lying on the driver's seat.

"Give it to me! You can throw it out the window if you want! I'll step back." There was a hysterical undertone in his voice. "Then I'll do it, I promise."

I took his cell phone in my hands. Mirko was throwing a fit outside. "Give it to me, Eva! You want to get out of here! You can't take it much longer! Think of your panic attacks! If not, you're going to crooooaaak in the car!"

His nagging made me nervous. I turned the music up so that I wouldn't have to hear him and scrutinized the little device, which was still turned on. Julian had a similar model, and so it was easy to find the feature where you look at saved pictures.

"You have no right! You're invading my privacy!" Mirko screamed himself into a frenzy out there. The more furious he got, the more I understood the cell phone's significance. He could no longer stop me from looking at the pictures, not with any of his rattling or shaking or knocking. After all, he hadn't respected my privacy, either.

The first picture, so the last picture that must have been taken, showed me—me standing in the dance club, white as a sheet, holding on for dear life to that bar table while the letter was being read out loud.

He had his eyes on me already back then?!

"What's this?" I turned the volume down on the radio, held the cell phone up against the window so that he could see the photo.

"I just wanted... You're like me! I know that from yo diary. Everything you've written could have been me wri it. When I read that you're writing everything down just so you can survive, that's when I thought, I'm doing the exact same thing! Except, you write, I take pictures! We have to fight back, Eva, you and I!"

"You're such an asshole, you're sick! You and I, we have nothing in common," I ranted and railed at him, so furious, so mad, that he stopped and slumped against the car, suddenly powerless. "I have always defended you in front of the others, Mirko, but now I know they were right! You are mean, deceitful…" *Sneaky*, is what I wanted to say, but I was able to stop myself.

He started crying.

"But only because they never wanted anything to do with me, because they've always excluded me, right from the beginning. They turned me into what I am today, that's why! All I'm doing is defending myself. You of all people should understand that. What about that girl during your school trip? You cut up her clothes, didn't you?"

"No, I didn't!"

"You don't have to lie on account of me. You can tell me what you won't even write in your diary! Come on, Eva, I'll understand! Every one of us has a worst secret!"

Good God, what was he talking about?

"I thought you'd understand, you'd be on my side! And what do you do? You're shutting me out, just like everyone else!"

How long would I be able to keep him locked out of the jeep? I had to keep our conversation going so that he wouldn't get any ideas about breaking the windows.

"I will take a look at the other pictures now, and then I decide whether or not I will let you back in."

Mirko's tears left streaky marks on the car door window. His fingernails scratched the glass with a muffled sound. He opened his mouth but didn't say a thing. Instead, he glanced through the window at the cell phone display, like a fish inside a fish tank.

First, there were a few pictures of his dad. Bernd looked the worse for wear: gray skin, sad, ill.

I shot Mirko a questioning glance.

"It was his own damn fault!" he whined and pressed his runny nose against the glass. "He shouldn't have gotten involved with her!"

"You mean Alina?" It was really only a rhetorical question, and Mirko, who now seemed like a pale, fishy wimp to me, didn't reply.

A girl's face in the next photo: not Alina, but Emra— leaving the girl's bathroom and looking as if she'd been crying. Did Mr. Sneaky here—and this was the first time I ever used this name for him—actually prefer taking pictures of sad, unhappy people?

"Emra is a stupid know-it-all, and you should see her brother, Hakan…"

"What was the story with Alina?" I interrupted him.

"Alina hated me, she messed with me all the time, she was one of the worst and meanest bitches, and my dad knew this, but he didn't care and kept messing around with her, kept rambling on and on about being in love. He doesn't give a shit about how *I* feel about the whole thing!"

My knees started shaking. Not bad enough for Mirko to notice, but still bad enough so that I realized I wouldn't be able to take it much longer stuck inside this car. It was to claustrophobic, too cage-like; there was not enough oxygen and too much horror inside of me.

The next picture was very dark, so I initially skipped it, along with the next two that were seemingly underexposed. But then I took another look: the school party.

I knew the picture. It was the picture Mirko had shown me before. Julian and Emra, standing together, taken at a later point in time when Bernd and Alina had apparently "already left."

It had to be the last one in the series he had taken of her and my boyfriend. For a long time I had only been interested in exposing Julian by way of these photos. But all I cared about now were the pictures that Mirko had taken *after* he had taken enough at the party, and *before* he had taken any of his grieving dad. Who had Mirko taken photos of in the middle of the night, in the dark? Outside. Possibly the same night Alina died.

Meanwhile, Mirko had gone quiet outside the car. I didn't dare to look at him; was afraid of what I might do, as if trapped in a nightmare; was afraid he could make me open the jeep's doors with a single evil look in his eyes.

I pressed the cell phone button that would show me the first of the two underexposed pictures again, the ones I had skipped before. It was gray and blurry. But you could make out trees, a face, a hand, white, held in front of a face. You could also see hair. The person trying to protect him- or herself from the camera's flash had a mop of curls, and there—part of an arm, a piece of burgundy-colored jacket.

So that was Mirko's secret!

I felt like I was tumbling down that steep, rocky slope a second time.

A moment later, I could hear Mirko's high-pitched voice close to my ear: "It's all his fault! If he hadn't brought her into the forest, if he hadn't left her by herself, nothing would have happened! I didn't do anything! I didn't touch her! She kept bitching about how he shouldn't trust me, how he should punish me for that website—she kept badmouthing me the whole, entire time. And what did *I* do? Nothing! One little prank, a few pictures—and all of it was true!"

I couldn't listen to this. I couldn't. If I only tried to imagine those moments between Mirko and Alina—Alina's final moments—I would go completely and utterly insane. I pressed my hands over my ears in desperation.

31

I had to get out of here. But how? Start the engine and drive? I had never driven a car before, and I didn't dare to now. I'd be better off drawing attention to myself. And hope that some other car—any car—accidentally took this little dirt road in the middle of the night. Nervously, I searched for the light switch, honked the horn.

"Stop it!" It had dawned on Mirko that I would never, ever open the car door if I could help it, and he lost it completely. He pushed and pulled on the door handles, tried the trunk, ran around the car, yelled profanities that were meant to intimidate me: "You're not going to make it, Eva! You're scared shitless in small, confined spaces; you're even scared shitless if someone is only staring at you!" He gave the tires and the car door a furious kick. Would he manage to break the windows with a rock or a wooden post? My heart was pounding. My breathing turned into panting. I couldn't just sit here and wait and risk him forcing his way in eventually. I needed something to defend myself with. Honking the horn with one hand, I used the other to search the glove compartment. Nothing but operating manuals and music CDs. Why hadn't Vollmer left his hunting rifle on the backseat?! And what about the travel bag?

I kept on honking and pulled the bag to me, rummaged through its contents: chocolate, sweater, canned food, two sleeping bags, two brand-new toothbrushes, shaving foam. Unbelievable! Had Mirko really planned on running away and abducting me?

All the way at the bottom was my journal. For a moment, I forgot about the situation I was in, let go of the horn, and opened the journal. Tears were streaming down my face: this bastard had annotated my journal entries, crossed parts out, added exclamation points in the margins.

"Yeah, go ahead, why don't you read all about how dumb you are!" Mirko grimaced from outside the window. "You are an unwanted piece of shit just like me. Nobody wants you! Not even your Julian wants you anymore, and you know it!"

He was now trying his hand at psychological warfare. His words were full of poison, his eyes full of scorn. I had to protect myself, had to close my ears and eyes, quick. I must not allow him to use this knowledge against me.

"Even your fox guy hates you! You're making him sick!"

I reached for the shaving foam.

"And your parents, they're ashamed of you!"

I don't hear any of this. I'm spraying the windows. That's my assignment, the only thing I'm focused on. Whatever he's saying out there, it doesn't concern me. He's wrong anyway. Mirko really only is a stupid asshole.

"Shit, stop that, that's my old man's car!"

The white, blue-tinted foaming gel has a surprisingly high yield and excellent adhesive properties. The mess I'm making can't really be called a protective shield, and it certainly isn't suitable for defense. But still, I feel like I'm defending myself, and I'm keeping Sneaky away from me, if only visually.

Sneaky—where did he sneak to? I don't see him any-more. While that was the whole idea, I'm suddenly wondering if he's even still nearby. The shaving foam clings to the glass like a damp, white blanket of snow. The insults have stopped, and I can't hear any steps outside because of all the honking.

I prick my ears, take a short break in between each honk attack: nothing.

I make an eyehole in the foam, stare through it like a medieval knight through a loophole. Except that I have no crossbow and my castle is a heap of metal.

Where was Mirko? Was he looking for something to smash the windows with? A heavy rock, some kind of a trail post? Had he already found a weapon and was closing in? Was it easier to smash the little windows back there than the windshield? Or the other way around?

I shift to the backseat, make myself another loophole. Foam gets into my eyes, I rub, squint, open wide my burning eyelids: nothing! I slide back into the front again. If I let go of the horn, nobody will find me and I'll be lost; but if I keep honking, I won't be able to hear anything myself, and I won't even see the attacker coming. I'm going crazy without 360-degree vision. The foam was a disastrous idea, only made the trap close around me faster. My breathing gets heavier. I'm out of options to take charge of my situation. What on earth should I do?

Rip open the door, make a run for the forest, run like I've never run before in my life? And what if that's exactly what Mirko is waiting for? What if he's right next to the car, lying in wait like a mountain lion waiting to get behind me as soon as I leave the car so he can pounce, strike? Or maybe he doesn't want to grab me at all but instead force me deep into the forest? Then he won't have to touch me and can wait until I tumble down one of the steep slopes by myself. Maybe that's how he forced Alina to her death? Without any physical force, just by using words—with the pure malice of a fearmonger.

I have to make a decision. I have to do something. I can't take this anymore. I know it's dumb to run into the forest, but my fingers are already reaching for the door handle. I can barely breathe in here, and the foam makes it even worse. One of the windows is going to shatter in a minute. I don't want to be a helpless victim in Mirko's hands. The least I should do is run.

On the other hand: A hunt. In high heels. No roads, darkness, brushwood. Stumbling, pushing on and on, looking for shelter. The abyss.

I can't do this!

But I need to get out of here!

How do you honk for your life?

How do you make a decision if both possible options might mean certain death?

Tormenting, seemingly endless moments of uncertainty. Checking through the eyeholes, over and over. While I'm keeping watch on my sticky cocoon and being locked in a state of furious conflict—which is becoming unbearable, like a fire burning inside of me—Mirko might be waiting out there, patiently waiting for my nerves to give way. What is my enemy thinking, "If she runs, I won't need to damage Daddy's car, and later on I can say that the crazy girl snapped and that she ran headlong into danger?"

This is a battle I cannot lose. I'm trying to remember something the fox guy taught me. I try to calm down, try to concentrate on things I can comprehend with my five senses: the film of cold sweat on my skin; the green LED lights on the dashboard clock—0:27; the horn that's thankfully still as loud as it was before; the smell of the shaving foam and how it runs down the glass in long, greasy drops; the taste of blood from my lip.

0:28.

I.Can't.Take.This.

Close your eyes. Breathe from your diaphragm. Count the seconds.

0:29.

Mirko is going to attack at any moment. I will hear a thud, beside me or behind me, and I'm going to think: This is it.

And what if I do run?

It's possible to wake up during a nightmare. There is a point in a nightmare where you know that you can get out it, if only you can wake up. In this case: not a chance.

0:31.

Five things: the rubber feel of the steering wheel under my honking hand; the lion patch on my denim jacket that my mom gave me because I'm a Leo and need to develop courage; the monotonous voice of the radio newscaster; the final hint of Julian's eau de cologne; the taste of blood in my mouth that little by little becomes boringly neutral again, after being all salty and iron-y.

0:37.

Mirko, you're going to lose this little war of nerves! All good things come in threes: my hands, soft but ready to defend myself to the last drop; my ears, acutely trained by now to notice even the faintest sound through all my honking; my will, still there and getting stronger by the minute.

0:41.

It seems like a miracle that I've been holding out for so long, me of all people! How is that possible? I'm sitting here with a clear and sober mind. I'm in grave danger, but I don't feel dizzy. Hey, Mirko, I'm not dying in here by myself, I'll just keep on living, and I'm even getting angry again.

By 0:43 I'm so furious that I—all the while honking the horn—shift over into the driver's seat, lower the window a tiny little bit, and scream, "Where are you, you little coward? If you come anywhere near me I will total your dad's car! I mean it! Maybe I'll do you a favor, Sneaky, and run you over first. You'll never get away anyway. They will get you! The police should be here any minute now."

I want to close the window straightaway, but I hesitate.

I can hear a miserable, pitiful sound. Mirko is still here, on this side of the car, very close. He's sitting next to the jeep on the ground and is bawling his eyes out.

Right then and there, I overcome all of my fears and limitations. I can hear myself say, almost daringly, "Mirko? What's up? You're not giving up on me, are you?"

He leaps up as if bitten by a snake; his fingers clutch the top of the open window.

"I didn't mean to, Eva, I didn't push her down that slope; she was freaking out, and she fell all by herself! It was an accident! It wasn't my fault! I didn't mean her any harm; I just followed the two of them into the woods because I wanted to know what they were talking about!"

I want to close the window, squeeze his fingers in, crush them, see him suffer, but I can't. He looks so pitiful and miserable. He is shaking and shivering, now that he's at long last being honest about what is coming out of his mouth. His sentences turn into stammering.

"He left her there by herself, and I wanted to get out of there too, follow him, talk to him. But then she saw me, and…" A heart-wrenching sob: "I didn't mean for it to happen!"

Would *anyone* want something like this to happen?

I'm recalling our encounters scene by scene: Mirko, at noon, out on the patio: likeable, timid, sad. Mirko, on the first evening, in the forest: lying on the ground in front of me. Isn't the first feeling that you have about an unknown person always the correct one? *Pity* is what I had felt.

But I also see Alina—or rather, what I remember of her. Her pale fingers wearing a ruby-red ring; she appears to be waving at me.

"I swear I didn't mean for it to happen!"

I sit there, and tears are forcing their way into my eyes— just like Mirko's fingers are trying to get into the car, like his words into my ears, his begging and pleading into my heart. And while my strength is leaving me, a voice deep inside is telling me that Mirko for sure isn't lying this time, that he really didn't want any of this to happen, that it was in fact impossible for this boy to be as mean as everyone always says he is; and this voice, this writhing, sneaky/debilitating voice, makes me reach for the door handle again with my fingers.

But then, just before I give in, I suddenly also see Midnight in my mind's eye. A cat doesn't know prejudice; it acts on instinct.

Look after myself.

Quietly, but still firmly, I say, "Take your fingers off the window, Mirko, I'm closing up."

Just at that moment, I hear the sound of an engine, and we're no longer alone on this dark, lonely parking lot by the Munkelbach Spring.

32

The first ones to arrive were Julian and Dustin on the Enduro dirt bike.

They grasped the situation right away. Dustin got ahold of Mirko; Julian pulled me from the jeep, embraced me fiercely, and asked me at least ten times if I was really alright.

"Yeah," I stuttered and reported in a few sentences what had happened.

Julian and Dustin took immediate action. Ranting and railing, they both started pounding into Mirko. Even though I was crazy furious at the boy who had almost really done me harm, I couldn't help but to try to pull them away from Mirko. "Stop it!"

"Call the police, Eva," Julian said. "He's going to confess by the time they get here."

"There's no cell phone reception!"

This piece of information made my rescuers even more aggressive. "Oh, that was brilliant of you, Sneaky, wasn't it," Dustin called. "I always knew that you were a mean, scheming bastard, but I had no idea you were this devious."

"Take good care of him and look after my girlfriend, Dustin." Julian got onto his bike. "I'll drive until I get reception, then I'll come right back."

He sped off, and for just a moment I was afraid that Mirko would try to make a run for it, now that there was only one opponent left. But he stayed there, lying on the ground, motionless, without defending himself—just like on my first evening in Munkelbach.

"Now do you see, Eva?" Dustin said to me. "You didn't want to believe that Sneaky here was dangerous."

"I wanted to make up my own mind."

He snorted in contempt.

"Under normal circumstances that might be the right thing to do. But to risk your life for it?"

I glanced over at Mirko, who lifted his head for a moment so that our eyes met.

"Well," I replied slowly trying to choose my words carefully, "despite everything, it was worth it. At least I wasn't biased against him from the start. Because that's one of the reasons he turned out to be the way he is. Although..." I felt a sudden urge to kick Mirko with my foot. "Although everyone else's behavior is no excuse for what you did, Mirko! You had every opportunity to choose a different path—just like me. Instead, you chose to hide behind your self-pity, and so you always stayed Sneaky."

I spat the last few words out more than I spoke them. And now I stood there, listened to my breathing, felt the blood throb in my temples. I was alive, and I loved myself, and I was still me, and I snapped at Mirko, "Just so we're clear once and for all: You and I have nothing in common! Nothing!"

Mirko squinted his eyes and turned away his face. Dustin seemed surprised. "Eva," he called out as I ran behind the car to allow tears of relief to flow freely.

Julian returned a few minutes later; then two police patrol cars entered the parking lot, followed by Laura and Mickey.

When I was at long last finished answering all of the police officers' questions and left the police station together with Julian, neither one of us wanted to return to the mill. Fortunately, the hotel opposite the police station was still open and had a room for us. But that wasn't really the solution. Although we were no longer in Vollmer's mill, Mirko, Bernd, and most of all Alina were so vividly present in my mind that I was unable to close my eyes without seeing any one of their faces.

When we left the next morning, the entire circle of friends was waiting outside the hotel to say their good-byes. I guessed it was Chris's idea, but I still shook everyone's hand and then told Julian in no uncertain terms that I wished to be taken to the railroad station.

"I can totally understand that you're dying to get out of here." Chris gave me a quick hug and then handed me a piece of paper with his address and phone number. "If you ever want to come back someday, or if you just want to call me sometime, that would be nice."

"We'll see," I replied. I would have liked to say something nice. I liked him, but I really didn't think that was reason enough by any stretch of the imagination.

I wasn't even sure when it came to Julian.

Shortly afterward, we were back at the railroad station and stood on the same platform I had arrived at four days earlier; we held hands, arms swinging like children, and looked at each other with a certain amount of regret.

"Can't we just go on another vacation, Eva? Pretend like this whole thing never happened?"

"It would be crazy if you could just rewind and re-do everything in life that didn't go too well."

"With most things, that won't work. But with us, life could make an exception, couldn't it?!" Julian beamed at me for the first time in a long time in the same way he had beamed at me when I first fell in love with him.

"We'll see," I said evasively and was glad when the train finally arrived.

Julian carried my backpack up into the compartment and waved like crazy. You should have made more of an effort before, I thought angrily, and only waved back once. So long, Munkelbach. I don't ever want to see you again.

Koblenz, Bonn, Düsseldorf. No delayed trains, in no mood to write in my journal. Everything different.

But shortly before I arrived, my dad called: "Eva, when exactly are you getting here? We've got a bit of a problem with the construction site..."

33

"No way!" The fox guy slapped his thighs in amusement. "Your parents didn't even come and get you? That must have been the icing on the cake, huh?"

"Yeah." I had to smile, even though I could never be sure whether he just wanted to lighten the mood with his joking around or whether he was pulling my leg. "Well, to be fair, they didn't know what had happened. When Julian and his friends were looking out for me on Saturday night, they didn't think of calling my parents. They suspected Mirko immediately. Because Olga, you see, happened to notice that I left the dance club in a hurry, and that I got into Mirko's jeep. Julian called the police. The cops must have made a connection between the Alina case and my disappearing, because Mirko's dad gave a statement in the morning, confessing that he had left Alina by herself in the forest by the castle ruins after they'd had a huge fight. And then they were back to that website. It was, of course, Mirko who had uploaded all those nasty pictures of Alina, and Alina wanted his dad, I mean her boyfriend Bernd, to punish Mirko or at least make him apologize."

The fox guy knitted his eyebrows in deep thought. And because I wasn't sure if he was still with me on all those new, unfamiliar names, I added, "Mirko had taken extra pictures at the school party. That started the whole discussion between the two of them up again. You see, Mirko is such a mean, devious, resentful person. The murder…"

And once again, I was wrong about the fox guy. He had listened attentively and immediately interrupted me: "If I understand correctly, it's not at all clear whether or not it was murder."

"Yeah, well," I said somewhat impatiently, because I didn't like this preliminary ending to the story one bit. "The police didn't find any evidence of foul play on Alina's body, and Mirko says he went into the forest on his mountain bike that night to listen to the two of them talking, and that he had scared Alina—but it hadn't been on purpose." Sarcastically, I added, "You see, Mirko never does anything on purpose. The poor boy was really only scared of his dad, didn't really want to eavesdrop, and maybe even wanted to apologize for the website story. And the same with me, of course. He only wanted to talk and, oh no, certainly not *scare* me when he wrote me that threat letter, took away my cell phone, drove into the forest with me!"

The fox guy nodded.

I was fighting back my tears.

"But it's all a lie, because why would he take pictures of Alina if he didn't mean to scare her? And why didn't he help her when she fell down that slope? Mirko couldn't have known that she didn't survive the fall. Shouldn't he have assumed that she had only hurt herself a little? Shouldn't he have gone for help? No matter how this all turns out, *I* know for a fact that Mirko is guilty, even if he never even touched her. He scared her, scared her so much that she panicked and ran, even though she definitely knew about those steep slopes. He tried it with me in exactly the same way when he realized that I would never understand him, that I wasn't like him at all. Even though I felt excluded, felt locked out for a long time, I never tried to take revenge. Instead, I always tried to change myself and tried to connect with people, tried to understand them. I never did anything to that girl during our school trip!"

"And I never for one second thought that you did," said the fox guy, and he said it in such a gentle, compassionate, and honest way that I started crying with relief uncontrollably. I was here, and I was safe and healthy, and all this horror was finally over.

"What do you think will happen to Mirko?"

"That's a good question." Dr. Fuchs looked at this watch. "There's what is called 'duty to rescue,' so he might be charged with that…"

The doorbell rang. It wasn't just this horror that was over: my fifty minutes were up, too. We were even running behind schedule.

"Well, we're going to have to talk about this next time, then." He, the one person I kept thinking about so strongly these past few days and who had no idea about this whatsoever, gave me a smile and got up, probably already thinking about his next appointment.

I shook his hand and left. I knew I wouldn't return much anymore. I no longer needed to.

Outside, the sun was shining; the sky was wide and blue, like you only see it during early fall; and somebody on the other side of the road was waving at me.

About the Author

Kristina Dunker was born in 1973 in Dortmund, Germany, and published her first book at the age of seventeen. Since then, Kristina Dunker has written a number of novels for children and young adults, and received several awards and scholarships, including the Literary Prize for Young Authors of the city of Voerde. She is a freelance writer based in Castrop-Rauxel and regularly holds lectures, discussions, and creative writing workshops for young adults.

About the Translator

Katja Bell was born in Germany and has spent most of her life living, working, or studying in Europe and the United States. She works as a freelance translator in Virginia, and is currently enrolled as a graduate student in the Applied Linguistics program at Old Dominion University, Norfolk, Virginia. Katja Bell has been translating professionally since the age of twenty; *Vertigo* is her first literary translation.